My Scandalous
Duke

D0810819

My Scandalous Duke

THERESA ROMAIN

Copyright © 2016 by Theresa St. Romain

Cover Design by Carrie Divine/Seductive
Designs

Image copyright couple © Period Images

This is a work of fiction. All names, places, and
events are products of the author's imagina-
tion or are used fictitiously. Any resemblance to
actual events, places, or persons, living or dead,
is entirely coincidental.

Chapter One

May 1801

London

The hardest part about telling her brother—*again*—that she was leaving his household was how much Eleanor wanted to stay. It wasn't every month a woman became an aunt for the first time.

But she couldn't keep borrowing her brother's family. Her brother's house. Not when she'd once had her own—almost. Not when she was determined to have them again.

"Don't be silly, Sidney," she said lightly, peering into the back corner of her just-emptied wardrobe. "You and Mariah don't need me around now that you've your firstborn to coo over. You'll have this whole wing full of nursemaids and tutors within the week."

Had she got all her gowns? Her shoes, her shawls? Surely she had, for they covered the bed and chairs in great spills of color. The scents of camphor and dried flowers filled the room, faint but unmistakable.

She pushed her unruly brown curls back, wedging her hairpins in more tightly. Packing was so much easier when her elder brother didn't send her lady's maid on some trumped-up errand, like the high-handed marquess he was. But never mind. She hadn't been Palmer's wife for five years and his widow for three without learning to do a few things herself.

"I doubt we'll fill the *whole* wing." Sidney, Marquess of Athelney, looked strained, though he managed a smile. "At least not until the baby gets old enough for a tutor."

Crossing the room to Eleanor's favorite wing chair before the fireplace, he tossed a shawl from its seat to the floor and flung himself into the chair. The day was fine and the grate remained unlit, but he stretched his feet toward the hearth from habit. "Ellie, I wish you'd stay. With Parliament in session for so many late nights, Mariah could use your company. She won't rise from childbed for at least a week."

Eleanor eyed the shawl, twining across the patterned carpet like a sleepy snake. "I know what you're doing. You're trying to make it even *more* difficult for me to pack."

Sidney gave her a smile that somehow blended innocence and diabolical cunning. He was far more fair than Eleanor, with well-behaved light hair and skin that tended to freckle, but when he wore this expression, the siblings' resemblance was unmistakable.

"You schemer. Well, it's not going to work." Eleanor sorted through the shoes on the bed, pairing slippers heel to heel. "I intend to remarry. I've wanted to for two years now, ever since I laid off mourning for Palmer."

"And you *can* remarry. Of course you can. Only, wait to go out in society until—"

"Wait until, wait until. Wait until what? There's always something to wait for." At her flare of impatience, the strained look tightened Sidney's features again, and she relented. "You must understand. How am I to find a new husband if I stay here with Mariah and the baby throughout the Season?"

Sidney had to allow the soundness of her question. "Even so. It's not right for a respectable widow to take lodging when you could be living with family."

Ah. About that. "I'm not exactly taking lodging, Sidney. I will be living at—"

"Ready to leave yet, Ellie?" A familiar handsome face appeared at the door to the room. "For God's sake, you have more clothing than a courtesan."

Nicholas Langford, the Duke of Hampshire, made free of Athelney Place, and no sooner had he spoken than he strode into the chamber.

The sight of her old friend always made Eleanor smile. "Hullo, Nicholas. I'm not even going to ask how you know how much clothing a courtesan has."

"I should think the answer would be obvious."

To cover a laugh, Eleanor blew an errant lock of hair away from her face. "Yes, well. Sarah has already packed away most of my things, but Sidney sent her to the fishmonger before she could finish my gowns and shoes." Most of them were old and out of fashion, but she'd got in the habit of not discarding anything that might be of use.

"The fishmonger?" Nicholas hooted. "Really, Sid, you could have thought of something more plausible than that. No one goes to the fishmonger at eleven o'clock on a Saturday."

Sidney ignored this, turning his lanky form in the wing chair to face the duke. "Wait. What's this 'ready to leave yet' question you fired at Ellie? Are you two going somewhere together?"

Brothers. So suspicious. Eleanor pasted on a smile. "As I was about to tell you, I will be staying at Nicholas's mother's house. Isn't that wonderful?"

Sidney declined to agree that it was wonderful. Instead, he frowned with the sort of force one could direct only at a sibling or a lifelong friend—and just now, one of each was on the receiving end of his annoyance. "Nick. This whole business of Ellie leaving Athelney Place was your idea, wasn't it?"

The duke raised his hands, dark brows lifting with mischief. "Ellie's idea. Completely. I swear, I'm innocent. I merely agreed that she might use my mother's house while that good lady is otherwise situated."

Since the death of her husband eight years before, Nicholas's mother had taken a string of lovers. The current one, an Italian count, had swept her away for the spring to flit about the Kingdom of Naples during a rare moment of peace.

The timing was excellent for Eleanor's purposes, for it meant that a fashionable house in Hanover Square was both unused and fully staffed for the London Season. Likely Nicholas could have rented it out for far more than the pittance Eleanor was able to pay him, but he insisted one couldn't put a price on helping a friend.

Or, better yet, on confounding that friend's elder brother.

"Come on, Ellie, chuck all your things into trunks." Nicholas yawned. "I'll accompany you over there and see you settled, then I'm going to Hampshire House to sleep for a week."

He did look tired, even more so than Sidney. Though her brother's light hair was tidy and his clothing fresh, Nicholas's black locks were tousled and his neckcloth creased. A shadow of stubble darkened his jaw.

"You're still wearing yesterday's clothing," Eleanor observed. "Just getting in from a long night of carousing?"

"I wish I were." Nicholas tugged at his cravat, looking rueful. "Yesterday's session of Parliament went ungodly late. Forty-four provisions in the newest enclosure act, and each bill has to be read over three times. And the speeches... I cannot speak of them, because surely they expended all the words in Christendom."

Sidney laughed. "I dozed off. Couldn't help it. My little namesake has spent every night of his new life squalling."

"I would have rather listened to a squalling baby than some of our illustrious peers." Nicholas crossed the room to swoop up the shawl Sidney had tossed to the floor. He stretched the cotton length out end to end, then began folding it into a small, tidy triangle. "Then, My Lady Skeptical, I went to White's to try to talk some sense into Addington and some of his Tory cronies. Oh, woe. They wouldn't listen to a thing I said until I sat down to cards with them, or so they said. So I tried a different strategy."

He turned his attention to the marquess. "Sid, did you know you can sneak a woman into White's if she wears a greatcoat and tricorn and a great deal of hair powder?"

"Everyone knows that," Eleanor scoffed. "So it wasn't cards you wanted to play after all. I suppose the Tories appreciated your efforts bringing in that costumed woman?"

"They ought to have. They listened to her far better than they did me. Though her conversation was probably less rigorous. I couldn't tell for certain. She conducted speech with each man, one at a time, in the private stairwell next to the card room."

Sidney looked surprised. "Not with Addington, surely? The Prime Minister is a measured man."

"Every man likes to show off his measure." Nicholas placed the neatly folded shawl into the bottom of a trunk that really ought to have been packed an hour before. "But no, Sid. You're correct. He's watching his step, since he has the double misfortune of succeeding Pitt and presiding over the first unified parliament of Great Britain and Ireland."

He really was quite good at folding clothing. Eleanor liked watching the play of his capable hands; unexpected, for a duke to perform a task so menial with such care. She tossed him another shawl, wanting to watch him fold it too. This was her favorite one, a heavy gold silk embroidered in intricate patterns of red and rust. It was new, a birthday gift from Sidney. She hadn't been able to afford anything so lovely for herself since the first year of her marriage.

"And how is that going? The unified Parliament?" Eleanor asked as Nicholas snapped the long shawl into a straight line. "Do you lords all sit shoulder to shoulder, borrowing each other's snuffboxes? Are there enough seats now that Irish peers have joined your ranks?"

Nicholas wagged a silk tassel at her. "Are you being flippant, or do you really want to know?"

"Of course I want to know. It's my government too." She eyed the trunk. To the devil with it; she'd tip all her shoes into there and let Sarah sort them out later. It wasn't as though they couldn't survive being packed away higgledy-piggledy. Most of them were worn beyond repair anyway.

"If only it *were* your government." Nicholas gave up on folding the slippery silk and draped it over Sidney's head. "The unified Parliament is like a marriage, I suppose. Constant negotiation, and more than a few battles over trifles. But invite a few women such as yourself into the House of Lords, and you'd have all the others quaking and rushing to obey your will."

She frowned, firing shoe after shoe from her bed into the trunk a few feet away. "Am I so terrifying?"

"Rather. It's that look you give sometimes. It makes one think what he's saying is utterly stupid. See? You're doing it right now."

"Save me," Sidney said. "I've been fixed with that look time and again ever since Ellie was born." He shook free of the gold shawl and tossed it away. It unfurled slowly, settling half inside the trunk and lolling over the side.

Nicholas stepped toward the trunk and shoved in the rest of the shawl. "You're not the only one with a sister, Sid. I have three, all older, and they are past mistresses of the scornful gaze." He looked up at Eleanor. "I do think Ellie's got them beat, though."

This conversation had gone in several unflattering directions already, and Eleanor still had gowns to pack. "Never mind all that." She tried to look saintly and calm as she tossed one last shoe toward the trunk. Not accidentally, she nicked the duke's knuckles with it. "So. Cards and a woman of pleasure, and the next thing you knew it was almost eleven in the morning. You are practically nocturnal."

"I am, but that's not all I did last night. Or ought I to say this morning? It was perhaps seven when I left White's; then I made one more call."

"Don't tell me about it," she sighed. He had been with a woman, no doubt. A woman of scandal and beauty and fashion.

In the three years since Eleanor had been widowed, she hadn't had much experience of any of these. Before her marriage, she had made a claim to the latter two. Palmer—the younger son of an earl, and a charming wastrel—had ensured their association with the first, until a heart seizure had carried him off with the same impulsiveness with which he'd lived.

The duke stood, looking ruefully at his wounded knuckles. "I won't tell you, because it was to do with a birthday present for you."

Her heart gave a little skip at these words: *for you*. It was good to be kept in mind.

Still, she groaned. "I thought you had given me the gift of pretending I didn't have a birthday last week."

"Nonsense. If I don't give you a present, then you won't give one to me. And I love presents. I regret that yours is late, but after this morning's meeting, I can assure you it will be ready soon." Nicholas was a year older than Eleanor, the same age as Sidney, and birthdays delighted him. When they were all children, they had always celebrated together.

But this year? Ugh. Eleanor would just as soon have ignored the whole matter of a birthday, for thirty sounded so much older than twenty-nine. A twenty-nine-year-old widow could flirt to catch a husband. Now that she was thirty, though? Thank the Lord, Sidney had agreed to dower her a second time. It wouldn't be nearly the fortune she had brought to her first marriage, but then, she wouldn't be nearly so reckless with her choice.

This time she would follow all the rules. She would marry the most proper, the stolidest, the most staid man possible. She would build a safe and respectable life. And her husband—and children, if she were granted some—would love her for it.

"I'll give you a gift for your birthday," she promised Nicholas. "In fact, I will give it to you early. When you squire me about, I'll help you find a wife."

This was a long-running joke between them, inevitably followed by his demurral. "Next year," he would say. He'd been saying it for a decade, since he was twenty-one.

But. This time, he said, "All right."

As one, Sidney's and Eleanor's heads snapped up. "What?"

Nicholas became occupied with folding one of the gowns strewn across the bed. It was a striped cotton in tones of gray, a dress Eleanor had worn when in half-mourning. "If you know someone perfect for me, Ellie, then of course I will marry her. I won't let the dukedom pass out of the family line."

Eleanor tried to take up a gown too, to echo the quick movements of Nicholas's hands. But her fingers were cold and slow. She ought to have had a fire lit, after all.

"Didn't think to hear you agree for a few more 'next years,'" she heard Sidney tease. He seemed to say it from far away.

"Why wait any longer?" said Nicholas, and he was far away too. "I know what marriage is—and what it isn't. I might as well marry someone meek and beautiful who will leave me alone to do what I wish."

What he wished. Lord spare her from the arrogance of dukes—or of younger sons of earls. Though in Nicholas's case, she knew from where his cynicism came. Eleanor had seen his parents play their only son off of one another for hostile years, until the death of his father freed his mother to seek happiness.

"That poor woman," she murmured.

"My future wife?" Nicholas held forth the gown, which he had somehow reduced to a small, tidy bundle. "She'll live in luxury. That's got to be worth something."

"Thousands a year, to be literal," said Sidney.

Eleanor took the folded gown from the duke's hand and placed it in the trunk atop her shoes. In truth, she'd been referring to Nicholas's mother, not to his nonexistent wife. "And what, pray tell"—she settled the gown in just the right place, wishing she had a few more shoes to throw—"does it mean to do what you wish, Your Grace?"

Nicholas snorted. "Right now, sleeping for a week."

"So you said earlier." She straightened, smoothing the skirts of her round gown with flat palms. "But you may not, for you're to escort me to a card party at Lady Frederick's house tonight."

He dropped the gown he had just picked up. "Did I really agree to that?"

"I'm certain you did."

"Was I drunk?"

A smile tugged at her lips. "A lady never tells."

"I was, then. Oh, Lord." With a histrionic gesture of despair, he dragged a hand through his hair. "Ellie, must we?"

16

"It'll be very proper. The sort of place where we'll both find the perfect people we seek."

"A card party?" He coughed. "Ah... I sincerely doubt it'll be what you expect."

"It will be fine." Eleanor darted a sideways glance at her brother, who sported an amused expression. "If other sources of entertainment fail, we can gossip about Sidney."

The marquess's smirk vanished. "Hullo, that's not fair."

"I can hardly wait," muttered Nicholas. "Ah, well. Perhaps I'll fall in love tonight and then I won't have to go to any more card parties."

"That would be efficient of you," Eleanor said lightly. "Though you'll have to keep squiring me about until I meet someone I want to marry. Unless you can get someone else to take on the dreadful task."

She arched a brow. He arched one right back.

She waited him out—and soon, he tugged a white handkerchief from his pocket and waved it at her. "Fine, fine. I surrender. I'll take you." He sighed. "I've read enough novels to know how that goes. Whoever spends time with you will inevitably fall in love with you."

What a warm day it was, wasn't it? Her cheeks felt flushed. She should have opened the windows. "You flatter me, Nicholas."

"And it'll likely be someone horrible," he continued. "With me at your side, I can make certain no one comes near you unless they'll make you a suitable husband."

Oh. Well. "You don't flatter me," she realized.

"I like that plan." Sidney nodded. "I'm worried about you, Ellie. Palmer... he wasn't good to you. I wish I could keep you safe."

Brothers. This was what his hesitation was all about. The fake errands for her maid, to slow her packing. The pleas to remain at Athelney Place a bit longer.

"I won't be any less safe at the dowager's house than I would be here," she said.

"She'll be safer," Nicholas replied. "The butler is an absolute terror, and the footmen are all former boxers. An eccentricity of my mother's."

"I'm not worried about her physical safety." Sidney looked strained again. "But..."

He trailed off, and she knew that there were too many words and not enough breath to speak them.

> *But I remember how carelessly Palmer treated you.*
>
> *But I remember how alone we were as children.*
>
> *But I'm afraid of you being hurt, and of me being alone again.*

Or maybe those were Eleanor's words. For Sidney wasn't alone now: he had a bright, sensible wife and a grumpy little week-old son. But for years after their parents had died—one of measles, one of influenza, and within three months of each other—Sidney and Eleanor had had only each other.

And Nicholas, whose family held the neighboring lands in Hampshire and whose boisterous household seemed to offer everything their lives were lacking.

"I'll be fine, Sidney." She smiled. "I promise."

Oblivious, Nicholas was tossing the remaining clothing from the coverlet toward the open trunk. "Three more gowns," he said, "and then we can close this trunk and have you on your way. Sidney, are you going to help your sister?"

Sidney's worried expression persisted for a moment—then he wiped it blank and said, "I rather thought I'd ring for a servant."

Eleanor propped her hands on her hips. "Ha! You mean you didn't send them all away on useless errands to thwart my departure?"

Humor touched his mouth. "Ah...no, only yours."

And so they finished the tasks at hand. In a few minutes, the clothing was stowed, the trunk was shut, and it joined the other boxes and trunks and valises and cases to be transported to Her Grace's residence in Hanover Square. It was near Nicholas's grand Hampshire House and a short trip from Sidney's home—a familiar part of London to Eleanor. Yet for all that, it felt like a momentous change indeed.

She stood then in the grand entrance of Athelney Place, watching Sidney's servants scuttle to and fro with her packed-up possessions. Nicholas joined her, a tall figure scented of the previous night's scotch and smoke.

"It's strange, isn't it?" he said.

"What's that?" She turned to look up at him.

"How quickly everything is changing." He shook his head, all puzzlement. "Sidney a father, you and I wanting to get married."

"Um." Her heart paused, as if to confirm it had heard correctly. "What was that?"

"Oh. Not to each *other*." He waved a hand with a careless laugh. "But separately. You again, and I ... for the first time."

"Right," she agreed. "I knew that was what you meant."

One might as well agree with a duke, because he would get what he wanted in the end.

He really wasn't right, though. This change wasn't sudden; it had been happening for years. He just hadn't noticed.

He hadn't noticed when, after three Seasons of wishing and hoping, Eleanor stopped waiting for him to fall in love with her.

He hadn't realized what a change it was for her when she wed the most flashy, dashing rogue in London. Adrian Palmer had made her laugh and forget. Nicholas had never known that she wanted to forget him.

He hadn't understood how much she'd tolerated after the first excitement of marriage was over. How straitened her life had been once the dowry was gone.

But then, she hadn't wanted him to know. And he was a duke, and dukes didn't have to notice anything they didn't wish to. They kept busy and yet more busy seeing to the needs of their tenants. Arguing in Parliament. Easing their leisure hours with food and drink and sex and gambling.

Nicholas was a very good duke indeed.

The scent of yesterday's eventful nothings on him—the smoke and drink, the arguments and flirtations that had accompanied them—were too strong, and she stepped away from his side.

A footman carried the last bandbox from the entrance hall. His footsteps echoed on the marble floor, ringing through the great empty space as if neither she nor Nicholas were there anymore.

"You're right," Eleanor said again. "How quickly everything has changed."

It hadn't yet—but she was determined that it would. Beginning that night.

Chapter Two

Accompany me to a card party, Ellie had said to Nicholas. *It'll be calm and quiet and amusing*, she said.

Ha. Ellie must have been out of society longer even than Nicholas had realized if she thought a card party would be a calm and quiet affair. They certainly could be amusing, though. At the last one Nicholas had attended, there were more guests than cards and more liquor than anything else. The women in attendance wore few garments, and the men few inhibitions.

Not exactly the sort of event at which one might obtain the perfect future spouse. But Ellie insisted, so they went.

The late-spring evening wore a veil of warmth and starlight, unexpectedly pretty as he accompanied Ellie into Lady Frederick's sprawling town house. When they reached the ballroom, yet more of the unexpected greeted him.

"I can't believe it." Arms folded, Nicholas regarded Lady Frederick's ballroom. "This really is a card party. For cards."

Cards, cards, and only cards. Tables and tables for play, scattered over the polished floor that ought better to have been used for dancing and revelry. Chandelier upon chandelier, holding scores of candles to wink at the dark sky outdoors. Quartet after quartet of men and women, laughing and conversing, yet intent on their games. A few others milled about the edges of the room, perhaps looking for an advantageous place to sit.

"Surely cards are required at a card party. Did you expect it to be otherwise?" Ellie hadn't left his side yet. Like Nicholas, she must be scanning the room. Looking for an empty seat, maybe—or a likely future husband.

"I did expect that," he admitted. Fondly, he recalled the quantities of liquor that had flowed at the last so-called card party. He had been looking forward to the liquor tonight, for this business of squiring an old friend about so she could find someone to marry was more than a little odd. It gave him a sort of protective feeling. As if he were as responsible for her choice as she was.

Ellie let her shawl fall from her shoulders to settle in a graceful drape at her back. Her blue gown was a pretty shade. "If you're intent on becoming drunk, I'm sure you could manage it. Look, the footmen are passing out wine."

Their hostess, a wiry widow of indeterminate age, was also circulating about the room—and looking as smug as a dog with a joint of mutton. Lady Frederick fancied herself a cornerstone of English society, and she must be pleased with the gathering she'd assembled. Mostly Tories, Nicholas observed.

"Forgive me for not greeting you at once, Your Grace! Lady Eleanor!" Their hostess beamed. From the twists of her drawn-back hair of a faded brown, pert blue plumes wagged. "Such a crush tonight—I can hardly credit it!"

Nicholas eyed the sedate movement of players to and from whist tables. "Indeed. I'm fortunate we could squeeze into the space."

Ellie cleared her throat. "I notice your decorations, ma'am. You are enthusiastic."

That was putting the matter mildly. For the occasion, her ladyship had draped every wall of the ballroom with the new Union flag.

"Those are to honor the king! England has conquered another country, and the best of Ireland belongs to us now!" Lady Frederick spread her hands, as if drawing in...well, entire countries, apparently.

"Not *quite* what was intended by the Acts of Union, ma'am," he replied. "But I am certain the king would appreciate the sentiment. When are you expecting him to arrive?"

"Oh, no—is he to come?" Ellie wrinkled her nose. "I'm dressed too plainly. I ought to have borrowed some of Mariah's jewels."

"Not at all," Lady Frederick reassured. "His Majesty is not expected this evening—as far as I am aware, though he would be most welcome! Do not worry yourself, Lady Eleanor. You are perfectly suitable. We are only a gathering of good Tories here, such as His Majesty would approve."

Good Tories. Grumble. "Even mere Whigs such as myself can appreciate the sight of the new flag, ma'am," Nicholas said.

Lady Frederick gave a peal of laughter. "His Grace is so *funny*!" she exclaimed to Ellie.

"He is," Ellie replied gravely. "I am so often beset by laughter in his presence that I have had to loosen my corset-strings."

The older woman's eyes went wide.

"Lady Eleanor is also funny," Nicholas said, speaking with the same sort of straight face Ellie had used. "As are you, ma'am. I much enjoyed your joke about the best of Ireland belonging to us now."

"Ireland? Was that humorous?" Lady Frederick lifted a hand to her throat.

"Oh, very. Because the Irish Catholic majority still cannot sit in Parliament. By the dictate of the king." He directed a small bow toward his hostess. "Surely the *best of a country*, as you put it, does not exclude the greater portion of its men."

"Or all of its women," Ellie murmured in Nicholas's ear.

"Therefore," he added with a bright smile, "I assume you were being satirical. Well done, madam. A clever jest."

"But if the king deems it preferable, then..." She trailed off, tugged between loyalty to the absent king and manners toward the present duke. "I am not certain... that is..."

Nicholas didn't entirely mind her discomfort.

"His Grace was just telling me how much alcohol he had consumed before accompanying me here," Ellie broke in. "He is completely inebriated. I hope you won't worry about anything he says, ma'am. Even dukes talk utter rubbish sometimes."

Oh, fine. At this unmistakable prompt, he relented. "That's true. Dukes do that." He couldn't resist adding, "Even the Tories among our number."

"If you insist, Your Grace." Lady Frederick maintained a smile, but her expression was glassy. She then excused herself to become lost in the so-called crush of her gathering.

"You are so funny," Ellie said gravely in the wake of that lady. "How funny you were just now."

Nicholas shook his head. "If she loves the Tory party so much, why am *I* here?"

"So that she might draw you into her web, of course, and suck the life from you."

His chin drew back.

Ellie flipped open a delicate ivory fan. "Nicholas. *Honestly.* She invited me because she thought I was lonely. Then I asked if I might invite you. And she allowed it, because strong political leanings and graciousness are not mutually exclusive." She eyed him with that you-are-an-utter-fool expression of hers. "Not *always*. Though in some individuals, they are."

"I do not mistake your meaning, you ungrateful woman." When Ellie pulled a face at him, he asked, "How long must we stay? There's no one fashionable here at all."

"Good," Eleanor said crisply. "I made the mistake once before of choosing a man of fashion."

Palmer, she meant. Nicholas frowned. The memory of Palmer always made him frown. "Let me reword. No one *useful* is here."

"Useful to your ambitions in Parliament, I suppose you mean?"

He shrugged. "You can't expect Great Britain and Ireland to mash themselves together into a united Parliament without some struggles."

"Rather like a marriage, didn't you say?" She tipped him a wink. "Nicholas, I'm proud of you. Only a year ago, you would have refused to accompany me. You'd have stayed out late with a woman in your lap."

"I held one on each thigh at Snodgrass's gathering last week."

He wished at once that he hadn't said it. Talking about such things to Eleanor didn't seem right. Not because she was a woman—although she *was*—but because she was a Pearce by birth. Her brother, Sidney, would have looked scandalized at the very sentence.

Eleanor didn't look scandalized, merely amused. "Some things never change, do they?" She waved her fan at him, wafting a sweet scent of something floral in his direction.

He drew in a deep breath. "And why should they? I can do as I please." He unfolded his arms and offered one to her. "Or I ought to be able to, but sometimes my friends drag me off to cursed dull occasions."

She settled a gloved hand primly on his forearm. "True friends introduce each other to new experiences. And the same is correct of romance as of politics: graciousness goes a long way."

"Are you seriously giving me instruction in courtship?"

"I would never!" She smirked. "Only, do not attempt to seat potential wives on your lap—at least, not upon first introduction. Now, shall we loom over a table of card players and attempt to join them?"

Nicholas agreed, and he and Ellie made their way around the room slowly, eyeing all the players. Ellie's eye seemed to be caught by one table in particular, where a middle-aged gentleman was finishing a hand of whist with an expression so blank his face could have been covered in paper.

Impatience flickered within Nicholas. "These aren't real games. No one is *wagering*." Absent were the piles of coins and bills and vouchers that filled the center of a card table during an interesting hand.

"Probably for the best," said Ellie. "Palmer lost what parts of my dowry he didn't squander at friendly card games just such as these. The stakes are high enough tonight, don't you think?"

"You mean finding a spouse, I assume."

"What else?" She nodded in the direction of Paper Face. "Do you know anything of him? Lord Barberry, is that not?"

Ha. He'd been right about her attention.

The realization didn't give him the satisfaction that being right usually did. "I know nothing against him," Nicholas granted. "He's been married before, of course."

"As have I. I can hardly fault him for that."

"The 'of course' is because he must be in his fifties. He could almost be your father." Nicholas paused, then added innocently, "His children are younger than you, though. By a few years. I think."

"Age doesn't bother me. I'm looking for a sensible man who won't be led astray."

"A sensible man isn't led anywhere he doesn't already wish to go."

"Then I don't ask for too much, do I?"

"You never could." This was the perfect truth.

She looked troubled. "Then...I am looking for a man I can respect and grow fond of. That is the sort of husband I will come to love."

She sounded so determined, as if saying the words could enflesh the theoretical husband and make the wished-for emotion real.

"You're describing an utter prig, Ellie."

She laughed. "A prig, you think? If it makes a man a prig to live within his means, to settle his debts without selling his wife's pianoforte"—Nicholas coughed—"then by all means, I seek a prig. I seek the sort of prig who won't stray from my bed"— Nicholas coughed again—"and who won't skimp on servants while throwing away guineas on entertaining friends. Count me among the prigs, Nicholas, and send just another such my way."

The color had risen in her cheeks. But she looked perfectly calm, and her wry smile never fell.

Still. He could tell that these words were momentous to her and that likely she'd been looking for an excuse to speak them. "That's me told, then," he said. "I apologize."

Her brows lifted. "I have a great deal of trouble keeping in mind all the things dukes do and do not, but surely apologizing is not one of them."

"The Duke of Hampshire never apologizes. But your old friend Nicholas does."

Her grin dimmed the candles. "Very well, old friend. You are forgiven." She returned her attention to the card table at which sat Lord Barberry. "There is a prig, as you put it, for me. And near him sits a sweet young lady who might do for you."

"Sweet, you say? I hope she is not *too* sweet." A woman lost her savor if she lacked a salty tongue.

"Oh, please! I know what a rogue you are. You want your own way all the time. You're no more interested in marriage to a spirited woman than I am in becoming the Prince of Wales's third wife."

Ah, Prinny, the king's dissolute first-born. He was a source of endless entertainment. "He'll take a third wife if he needs to. And I'll take a first."

It wasn't that he wasn't looking forward to contracting a suitable bride. It was just... yes, all right, he wasn't looking forward to that at all. A courtship, ideally, should be swooning and romantic. Instead, this was just another task to be ticked off his endless list, much like "persuade Addington to simplify the enclosure act" and "don't tell Sidney his baby resembles a crumpled drawing of a cabbage."

At least he had Ellie with him. An old friend to joke with and make this whole business more pleasant.

She looked up at him just then. Her next words were tentative. With a quick glance toward Lord Paper Face, a surreptitious smoothing of her skirts, she whispered, "Do I look all right?"

A dangerous question, asked for unknown and likely nefarious reasons. He had best answer carefully.

"I recognize that golden shawl," he offered. "I put it on your brother's head earlier, did I not?"

"You did." She took up the fabric's trailing end. Her fingers played with the smooth fabric, bunching it, then pressing it flat again. "I think it suits Sidney better than it does me, but it's the prettiest thing I own."

He couldn't disagree. Her dress was
not unattractive, but it was hardly in the
first stare of fashion. Still, it was a color,
and it was nice to see her in color. He'd got
used to seeing her in mourning clothes.
Plain and jetty, they bled the color from
her face and made her look wan. Or maybe
she had truly been wan, and now the idea
of finding a new husband was returning
the glow to her cheeks.

Lord Paper Face had played out his
hand, and he was looking over at Ellie.
Intent, evaluating. Dark eyes and a sharp
blade of a nose.

Nicholas could understand the man's
scrutiny, for Ellie was pleasant to look at,
slender and poised. Her gown was high-
waisted, a light blue silk with a sash. The
bodice was cut low, a darker blue silk that
framed her breasts.

Should one think the word *breasts* in
connection with a friend? Especially a
friend one had known since long before
that person had been possessed of breasts?

To hell with it. Eleanor looked damned
fine, breasts and all.

Not that he would put it to her in that way. He had already hesitated too long, and she was eyeing him with suspicion. "What's amiss?"

"Nothing, nothing. You look lovely," he said. "Though your hair looks strange."

Her mouth fell open.

But it was *true*. Her hair *did* look strange. And she *had* asked.

If there was one feature that had always defined Ellie for Nicholas, it was her hair. Ever since her girlhood, Ellie had cursed her riotous brown curls. They frizzed and twined and kinked and got in her face as she ran, huffing and indignant, behind the older boys.

She had looked forward to coming out in society, but when she did, she had never looked right to Nicholas. Not with her hair powdered fashionably pale and starchy, tortured into a puff at the front and long stiff ringlets at the back. The restraint of her hair had shortened her steps, shallowed her breath. A girl with such hair could not move with abandon. Until the end of a ball, maybe, or the twirl of a country dance, when he saw her at a distance haloed by candlelight, and she was laughing and her hair was starting to shrug free of its pins and pomades, rioting into springs.

But that had been more than a decade ago, and fashions had changed. Gone were the hair powder and women's stiffly boned bodices. France had had a revolution of its own, and once a tenuous peace had returned, no one could be bothered to get dressed again in panniers and powder and patch.

Nicholas had been more than glad to toss aside his hair powder and lop off his queue. His dark hair was thick and short and tousled.

And Ellie's? Tonight it was smooth, as sleek in its crown of plaits as if it were heavy silk, and she was just as much not-Ellie as she'd been in her first Season when she wore a toy boat atop her grandiose powdered hair.

It was the correct answer, to say her hair looked strange. But he knew it had also been the wrong one.

"I shall pretend," Ellie said from beneath her cap of fashionable hair, "that you did not say that. My hair looks perfectly acceptable. I can see it in the glass over there."

Turning to face him, she narrowed her eyes. They were green—not that he could see their shade in the candlelight, but he knew it well. He had been glared at by those green eyes many a time—though never, perhaps, with quite so much force.

"I can't imagine why you're being so disagreeable," she said.

"I can be far more disagreeable than this."

"That is certainly true." She rolled her eyes. "But Nicholas, you *said* you were interested in taking a wife. Look about you. Don't you see anyone you might deem...perfect?" She spoke the last word as though flicking a barb.

"Nobody is perfect," he grumbled.

"Perfect for your purposes, then. Meek and mild and beautiful. If you don't have any ideas, as I said, I've spotted someone who might do."

Someone who might do. Hardly romantic, but then, his blue-blooded parents must have chosen each other for no stronger reason than that.

Not that theirs had been a love story, or even a successful match at all.

With one hand on his arm, somehow Ellie managed to drag him toward... damnation, yes, toward the table at which Lord Barberry was seated. It was a table for four—and as Ellie and Nicholas approached, all four players sprang to their feet.

Greetings followed. Besides Lord Barberry, there were a couple of similar age to him—a Mr. and Mrs. Lewis, relations of the powerful Earl of Benwick—and their daughter Lavender. Ellie knew the Lewises and handled the introductions with a friendly ease that made Barberry's eyes glitter, shadowed and greedy. Ellie didn't notice. How could she not notice such presumption?

Mr. and Mrs. Lewis seemed particularly interested in meeting Nicholas. Lord Barberry seemed particularly interested in Ellie.

Lavender Lewis seemed particularly interested in her toes, blushing and shy as her parents twittered about needing to get refreshments, and would *dear* Lady Eleanor keep an eye on their *darling* girl, and *would* His Grace care to partner Miss Lewis for the next hand of whist?

And so the four of them—two would-be couples—were left with a deck of cards and a table bare of distracting vouchers and chips.

"What have you been wagering?" Nicholas asked. "There cannot be a proper game of cards without a wager."

Ellie, sitting at his left, kicked him under the table.

Lord Barberry looked up from handing out the cards, thirteen per player. "We have been wagering information." His dark eyes were shrewd. With his silver hair cut short and modish, he looked younger than Nicholas had expected.

"What sort of information?" Ellie asked. "I must leave it to you gentlemen to deliver state secrets unto us ladies. But what could we tell you in exchange?"

Her voice sounded higher, breathier than usual.

Barberry beamed at her. "I could think of many things, Lady Eleanor, that I would be enchanted to have you tell me."

"How about favorite flower?" Nicholas blurted. When three sets of eyes flicked his way, he explained, "The winning lady could reveal her favorite flower. Surely we gentlemen could make use of that information."

Across the round table, Miss Lewis met his gaze for a moment, then looked away again. She was very young, perhaps twenty, and dressed in pale colors that made her look more than ethereal, almost ephemeral. A promising quality in a wife who would be beautiful and meek: she would simply melt away when one hadn't need of her.

Guilt caught him at the thought. Would he be treating his wife, in that case, any better than his father had treated his mother?

He hoped her favorite flower was not lavender. Though fragrant, it was such a spindly flower. What did it symbolize? His sisters had used to dissect every arrangement given them by beaux, teasing out the secret meanings.

He couldn't remember. But no matter. This particular Lavender represented what he said he wanted in a wife, and so as if to atone for his lowering thoughts of a moment before, he bowed over her hand—currently holding thirteen cards—with scrupulous politeness. And then the game began, with clubs the trump.

For a game of whist, it was indifferently played. Miss Lewis was sloppy and shy, overlooking her hand's trumps in order to follow suit. Lord Barberry spent as much time looking at Ellie as he did at his cards. And Nicholas had to study them all, to make sure he knew what was what. It was more than a little distracting.

He played his final card, a low off suit, with a curse.

"Better for you we didn't wager any money, Your Grace." Lord Barberry smiled. "Lady Eleanor, as we've won, I believe you owe us a flower."

As the older man tidied the cards into a neat stack, Ellie tapped her chin in thought. "It is terribly uncreative of me, but I believe my favorite flower is a rose. I am sorry. I ought to have said something wild and inconvenient, to be fascinating."

"You could not fail to be fascinating," said Barberry.

Oh, please. A reply more pat could not have been imagined.

"My apologies, Miss Lewis." Nicholas had a few manners up his sleeve as well. "I was not a skillful partner to you."

"You were perfect, Your Grace." She fluttered, drawing forth her gloves as if she wanted to cover her hands, then setting them aside again. "I fear I am not accomplished in this sort of play."

Was there a double meaning to her words? Perhaps, perhaps. She was blushing again. She really was quite pretty. Like a watercolor.

"Perhaps a drink before we play again?" offered Barberry.

"I ... no, I'd best not." Nicholas pressed his temple. "I haven't slept for a day. Strong spirits would knock me flat."

"I thought you had planned to sleep for a week." Ellie's brows lifted. "Or at least the afternoon."

"So I did, but someone whose name rhymes with Lady Belinor Balmer had a detrimental effect on my proposed schedule."

In truth, he had known he would doze for a few minutes at most. The wish to sleep for a week was as vain as any other deeply held wish, such as the one he'd once held for parents as devoted to each other as Sidney and Eleanor's parents had been before their early deaths.

Even when he had the chance to sleep, he usually ... didn't. He lay in his bed, thinking of all the things he could be doing, and with whom. His thoughts were a careful wall against the claws of those *other* thoughts. The alone sort of thoughts, in which he had a city full of acquaintances but few true friends. A dukedom that took away his choices about how to order his life. The memory of a silent dinner in the nursery as his parents dined in cold formality with the people one ought to know, not the people with whom one cared to spend time.

But damn it all, he was a duke. And those thoughts *belonged* behind a wall, because in front of it, he could do what he pleased, with whom he pleased, when he pleased.

"Never mind what I had planned," he said, taking the cards from Lord Barberry and giving them a quick shuffle. "If you're all prepared, let's play another game."

Chapter Three

The following afternoon, Eleanor returned from a visit with Mariah and the sweet-sleeping infant viscount, determined anew to create the sort of family she wanted.

That morning, Lord Barberry had sent over a clutch of pink roses, little delicate things on fragile stems. When she'd said she liked roses, she meant *roses*. Big, vivid, lush blooms. Thorny, strong stems. But she hadn't specified the sort she preferred, and the gesture from his lordship was kindly meant. Pink roses represented admiration, and that was a fine foundation for a courtship.

She had half hoped Nicholas would send some flowers as well, but nothing had arrived from him.

She could guess why. He had been wittily ungracious to their hostess the evening before, a trick that often delighted him—but only him. He was probably miffed at Eleanor for pointing out his poor manners. And it wasn't as though flowers from Nicholas would mean anything more than a friendly gesture at the best of times.

Ah, well. She handed off her pelisse and bonnet to a footman, batting ruefully at the curls that sprang down from their confinement to tickle her forehead and nape.

The footman bore the bent nose and flattened ears of a former pugilist, yet wore the dowager duchess's livery with grace. He was far better dressed than she was, with her drab-colored gown and gloves of plain cloth, but the butler had the staff too well trained to appear to notice this.

It was odd but pleasant, living in this house. She had done the right thing to leave Athelney Place.

Except now she would be alone, save for the house's staff, for the rest of the day.

Perhaps she'd visit the library and see what sort of books Nicholas's mother collected.

"My lady." The footman spoke in a broad accent. "His Grace awaits you in the front parlor."

Eleanor paused in the act of drawing off her gloves. "His Grace? You mean ... Hawthorne?" What was Nicholas doing here at this hour? It was too late for callers and too early for tonnish gatherings.

At the footman's affirmative, she handed him her gloves and made her way through the entrance hall toward the first door on the right. Before she could open it, Nicholas sprang out of the room with a grin on his face.

"Finally! You're here!"

"I'm here." His puppyish excitement was disconcerting. "Why are *you* here? This is my house. You aren't to be breaking in at all hours."

He grabbed one of her hands. "Actually, my dear fusspot, this is my house. And I'm here because your birthday present has been delivered. Come and see!" He all but dragged her through the doorway, her boot tip catching the edge of the room's stretching carpet and making her stumble.

As soon as she righted herself, she froze. "That's not my birthday present."

"It is." He stood next to her, practically vibrating with glee. "What do you think?"

At the center of the blue-papered room, it shone dark and lovely. Cautiously, hesitantly, she approached the gift. "It's...but, Nicholas. It's a pianoforte."

This was understating the matter. This was not merely a pianoforte. It was the sort of instrument whose name ought to be written in all capital letters, or pronounced with the formality of the script on the nameboard. *A. Pianoforte*. A grand one, its finish satin-smooth, its lid open and inviting: *let us make music*.

Her vision blurred. "I cannot believe it. It is too much."

Even as she said the words, her hand reached for it. She traced the edge of the music stand above the keyboard, the perfect height. Oh, it was all perfect. Even the scent of it, of cut wood and varnish. She breathed in deeply, sinking onto the accompanying bench seat.

Nicholas stood beside her. "You've made your token protest. Now I'll reply that it's not at all too much, and Palmer was a beast to sell your pianoforte, and the cost is as nothing to me." He poked at a key. "I'd rather not have to say all that, because it diminishes the glory of my gift. Could you oblige me by simply saying that you adore the gift and think it's the best birthday present anyone has ever given you?"

She wiped at her eyes with the back of her hand, then settled herself squarely before the keys. "Yes. I adore the gift. I ought to protest more, but I don't want to. I only want to play it." Her throat caught as she added, "It is truly the best birthday present anyone has ever given me." She looked up at him, standing so tall by her side. "It is the best gift of any sort."

He laughed. "You needn't go *that* far."

"But it's true." She spread her fingers over the keys, not yet pressing them. "Is this what you saw to yesterday morning? You were harassing John Broadwood as soon as the sun came up?"

"It was at least an hour after the sun came up, but yes, Broadwood needed a little harassing. He was supposed to have it ready for your birthday. He and his son were lucky I didn't put spies on them."

Her last pianoforte had had natural keys of ebony, with ivory slivers forming the sharps and flats. This instrument had reversed the materials of the keys, and the keyboard seemed to stretch endlessly as a result. Eleanor leaned forward to touch the highest and lowest ivory keys with her fingertips. "Look how large it is! What is the span—five and a half octaves? No, it's fully six!"

"It is six," he said proudly. "You shall play the highest and the lowest notes in London. Well, you and everyone else who has a pianoforte of this size."

She touched a key at the upper end; it tinkled like the ringing of a high bell.

Sliding a forefinger down the keyboard, she pressed each key lightly, stroking the ivory.

Could she feel the vibration of each struck string crossing the soundboard, or was she only imagining that she could feel the heartbeat of the instrument?

At the lower end, the notes grumbled and growled in a quiet thunder. Back up again, and the notes rang clear and sharp.

"It sings," she said. "Like a person, it sings. I have never played a grand pianoforte before."

Only the small square sort, which hummed along pleasantly. But this? Oh, it opened its heart to her. A heart of woods soft and hard, unfinished and glossy.

"This really is yours," Nicholas said. "You're to have it when you leave."

She lifted her hands at once. "Am I leaving?"

"Well, when you get married." He leaned closer to her. Today he smelled of soap and clean cloth. She shut her eyes for a moment, breathing deeply. "The butler told me Lord Barberry had sent you flowers."

Her eyes snapped open. "He did, yes. They are in my bedchamber now."

A falsehood. In truth, they were in the library. The flowers, and the accompanying note of scrupulous politeness: *With highest regards, & c.*

Deliberately, Nicholas placed three fingers on low keys and bashed a dissonant chord. "You'll soon be bored with him."

Pale pink rosebuds were pretty. Admiration was a fine sentiment. "Why do you say so? Because he's not scandalous like you?"

"Am I scandalous?" Nicholas perked up.

"Let me think." She tucked a wayward curl behind her ear. "Bringing a woman into the stairwell at White's?"

"I wasn't in the stairwell myself, you know."

"Two women on each thigh at... whose party was it?"

"Snodgrass's. And it was only one woman. On each thigh." He frowned. "Does that sound more interesting than 'two on my lap'?"

" 'Interesting' is hardly the word for it," Eleanor said dryly.

"Then I suppose I am scandalous, rather. Here, budge over and let me sit with you if you aren't too scandalized." He sat beside her, hip pressing against hers.

Time and time over the years, they had sat next to each other. But this—hip against hip on a seat almost too small for the two of them—felt startlingly near. Within her boots, her toes curled.

"Did you send flowers to Miss Lewis?"

"I did. Lavender."

Of course he had. "How unoriginal."

He laughed. "Not the *flower* lavender. Other kinds of flowers that are lavender in *color*."

"Oh." She shifted to the side, putting a small space between them. "That is rather clever."

"I do have those moments occasionally." His fingers moved slowly over the keys, testing their pitches.

"Do you want to play a duet?"

"No, no. I only know a little. I wanted to learn when I was a child, but I wasn't permitted."

Why was it his hands were so intriguing? Whether folding a scarf or dancing over an instrument, she loved to watch their deliberate movements. Surely they would move with the same certainty over a woman's skin.

Her toes had not yet managed to uncurl. Desire threatened to slip its bounds, and she had to hold it back. This pianoforte, glorious as it was, came as a gift from a friend. The man whose leg brushed against hers was a friend.

A friend who had sent lavender flowers to a pretty woman a decade Eleanor's junior.

Her toes relaxed.

"Why were you not allowed to play?" She sounded credibly calm and curious.

"Future dukes shouldn't be wasting their time learning the pianoforte, or so my father told me." He played an arpeggio, looking pleased at the sound thus created. "I was encouraged to play instead with lead soldiers or a globe."

"Better to become vainglorious than musical, then." When he laughed, Eleanor added, "I am beginning to wonder if dukes can do whatever they like after all, as you insist."

He shoved back with one foot, putting the small bench off-balance. "Of course they can. Or I can. I couldn't then, because I wasn't a duke yet."

She braced herself with a hand against the nameboard above the keys. "If you would like to play now, we could manage a simple duet. What do you think?"

Thump went the front legs of the bench, settling squarely again on the carpet. "I've no doubt you can manage your part and mine together. What shall I plunk out?"

"Put your hand here...just here. That's right." She guided his hand. It was broad and strong, and the simple touch of skin to skin made her bite her lip. *Friendly. Casual.* "Press with the thumb and the small finger."

"Ellie! I know the names of the notes." He drew his hand away, settling it where she indicated.

She blushed, but he didn't seem to notice. "Thumb on C, then. And I'll take the melody."

It was old and familiar, the song she chose. It had come to her mind as a simple one, one that would let Nicholas key with his left hand while she carried the tune.

But it carried her instead, its steps lilting and dropping, as she remembered the words of the country song.

I sowed the seeds of love,
It was all in the spring ...

So she had once, and she'd then lost.

"*The willow tree will twist,*" she whispered, "*and the willow tree will twine.*" Her left hand lifted to the keys, then she drew it back.

"It is a beautiful piece," said Nicholas. "Will you sing it?"

"It's melodramatic. A tune from the country, about love and loss. Aren't they all?" She tried to laugh.

"Sing it anyway, Ellie. I haven't heard you sing for years. Here, I'll get out of your way so you can play properly."

She thought he would stand—but he didn't. He only pressed over to one side of the bench. When Eleanor slid to its center to take both parts of the song, they were side by side again, so close that her left elbow was almost pinned between them as her hand rested on the keys.

Shyness seized her. Singing was even more private than playing, and she had got out of the habit of both. Yet she *wanted* to sing for him too, as she'd often done before they were grown and the business of being a man and a woman, a duke and another man's wife, had driven a distance between them.

She wanted to sing. She wanted to sing *this* song.

She began quietly, slowly, with the lines she'd recalled first. Her voice felt tight. She had not limbered it in song for a long time.

> *"I sowed the seeds of love, it was all in the spring,*
> *In April, May, and June likewise when the small birds they did sing."*

"You can tell it's a country song," Nicholas observed, "because the birds sing. London birds only cough and choke on coal dust."

She caught him in the ribs with her left elbow, winning a laugh from him before she sang on.

"My garden planted was with flowers everywhere;
I'd not the liberty to choose the flower I loved dear."

As she sang the next lines—rejecting the lily, the pink, the violet offered by the song's gardener—she prickled with awareness. He was beside her, watching her, listening to her. To play and sing like this, honestly and with passion, was to bare herself. In a way unfathomable with anyone else, anyone she knew less well.

"For in June there's a red rosebud, and that is the flower for me,
For oft I have plucked the red rosebud till I gained the willow tree."

"You don't like buds, though," Nicholas said quietly. "You like the big roses. The redder the better, with golden pollen at their hearts."

Her fingers paused on the keys. "You must stop interrupting. You are marring the wonderful musical experience I'm attempting to create for you."

"Apologies, apologies. Play on, my lady."

So she did.

"The willow tree will twist and the willow tree will twine,

I wish I were in that young man's arms that once had the heart of mine."

He was sitting so close to her, too close for ease. As she sang, she wished he would interrupt her again.

"... in the midst of a rosebud there grows a sharp thorn there."

He was quivering with suppressed words, one knee jouncing up and down.

She lifted her hands from the keys. "Go ahead, say it. You're about to fall over with eagerness."

"A rosebud with a thorn in it? What a monstrosity. The center of a bud is the *last* place a rose would grow a thorn. This song offers bad botanical teaching."

"What on *earth* do you do at a musical party when you are required to be silent while the musicians perform?"

"I usually don't listen."

"How lowering. I can stop playing anytime." *Please, please, don't tell me you want me to stop playing.*

"I believe that you can. You have already done so several times. But please don't stop again on my account."

She smiled. "Very well.

"I told him I did take no care until I felt the smart,

For oft I've plucked at the red rosebud till it pierced me to the heart.

I'll get me a posy of hyssop—"

"What *is* hyssop?

"It's a ... sort of minty thing. It's symbolic of becoming pure, I think."

And then she finished the song:

"... no other flower I'll touch,
    That all the world may plainly see I
loved one flower too much ...

    Come, all you false young men who
have left me here to complain,

    The grass that once was trampled
underfoot, give it time, it will rise
again."

She indulged in a little trill at the finish. What a treat to play keys of such fine ivory.

Nicholas touched the lowest key, but did not press it. "You may insist you want a proper husband, Ellie, but you play and sing as if there's a scandal in you waiting to get out."

Oh, if he only knew the decadent twists of her thoughts. "Wasn't my first marriage enough of a scandal?"

"Was it? Yet you wish to have him back."

She turned her head to look at him, so close they were almost eye to eye. "What, you mean the bit about the 'young man's arms' and him once having my heart and all that?"

His jaw tightened. His nod was short.

He had no idea about her heart; he never had. She adopted a dismissive tone. "That was only a song, Nicholas."

It wasn't, of course, and they both knew it. Palmer had taken her in his arms, and she'd once given him a piece of her heart. If he had been who she imagined him to be, he would have it still. She had drawn the veil before her own eyes, willing and wild.

But Palmer wasn't the one about whom she'd been singing.

"*Give it time, it will rise again,*" Nicholas mused. "Sounds rather lewd, that."

She choked, drawn at once from her willow-wound thoughts. "It's meant to be a profound image of hope and resilience."

"If that's what you have to tell yourself so you don't blush while you sing it, go right ahead."

She laughed. "You can't make me blush anymore."

"I should like to try."

It was difficult to hold his gaze, but impossible to look away. Was he joking, or...what did he mean? Her fingers tingled, a sweet echo of the twist of awareness through her body. How dark his eyes were, and how shadowed, and how she wanted them fixed upon her.

She moistened her lips. "What...what do you mean by that?"

"I would see you happy all the time, Ellie. Happy and blushing and laughing."

Oh. "That sounds pleasant," she replied. "Though not realistic."

"Which," he asked quietly, "is your favorite part of the song?"

"Oh...it's difficult to say. It has a pretty melody, I think. But if you're asking about the words, I don't care for the verse about the gardener, and how the singer asks him to pick the flowers."

"It's meant to be a profound image," he mimicked, "of hope and resilience."

"It's not, though. The gardener picks flowers that stand for qualities no one much cares about. Violets for modesty, lilies for purity, pinks for... I don't know what."

He looked thoughtful, breaking their gazes to fiddle with the hinge of the music stand. "What does lavender represent?"

"It's not in the song."

"I know. I was only wondering."

She could guess why. "It means the same sort of quality. Good qualities, I mean. Like purity and silence. And modesty, maybe?"

"Good qualities, you say?" The corner of his mouth curved. "You just said no one cares for them."

She lifted her hands. "I shouldn't have said that. They are fine qualities. Undervalued qualities."

"You and I don't undervalue them, though. We both want them in a spouse, do we not?"

She looked at her hands, ringless. They weren't as smooth as they'd been when she was younger. They were thinner now, and the knuckles were strong.

She did want those qualities in a spouse. She *did*.

But she didn't want *only* those qualities.

"Then," Nicholas added, "you chose the red rose for love. How did it go? *In June there's a red rosebud, and that is the flower for me*?"

"That is what the song says. I was singing a song. That's all."

"Right, the song. Well. It's May, so you haven't long to wait."

She didn't bother protesting again.

He fell silent—then blurted in a rush, "Why now, Ellie? Why do you want to marry again? Men are beasts. Bears and wolves and... oh, something dirty and careless."

This seemed ludicrous, sitting beside him as he was impeccably dressed, skin clean and lightly scented with spice, touching the ivory keys as lightly as if he feared to wake them.

"A wild boar, maybe?" she replied. "You are harsh upon your sex."

"I just don't know what a proper husband would have to offer a woman like you."

"What, precisely, is 'a woman like me'?" She moved closer to him again with the excuse of smoothing her skirts. "I probably shouldn't ask. I probably don't want to know what you mean by that."

"Nothing bad. Only good. What I mean is that you're a woman with everything you need. Independence. Enough money to live. Friends, family, intelligence. A damned fine pianoforte."

"But I don't have a family," she said. "And that's what I want. Sidney and Mariah are creating their own family now. Aunt is a nice enough title, but it's only a courtesy."

"You want to marry so you can have a baby?"

I want to be loved. "I would be glad to have a baby." It hadn't worked out with Palmer, more than once. Sadly. Each time, there was another reason for him to drink and flee.

"You don't really want a husband, then. You want a stud."

"Remember that look you said I gave you? When whatever you're saying is foolishness? Behold, Nicholas. You are on the receiving end of it now." She paused. With a crash of fingers on keys, she added, "Wait. What you just said is what *you* want. You want to marry someone who will give you heirs and leave you alone."

He went very still. After a long moment, he slowly stood. "You are terrifying, Ellie. You see far too much."

"Is that an admission that I'm right?"

He shook his head, but the curve of his lips made it other than a denial. "Play some more." He crossed to the long sofa that spanned the space between two windows. "I'm going to close my eyes, but it's not because I'm bored."

"Oh? And what am I to think, then, if my presence puts you to sleep?"

"Think that it's nice." He sat on the hard seat of the sofa, then leaned to one side, resting against a silk cushion. "It's nice, hearing you play. Being..."

He was mumbling by then, prostrate with the boneless fatigue of the exhausted.

And what *was* she to think of that?

She didn't know. But he wasn't wrong, altogether. It was … nice. Being here, in this lamplit room, just as if they belonged together. Being right about what he wanted, even as she was unsure about herself.

She had asked for roses, and she had received them: pink roses, admiration. Sent *with highest regard*. If she had what she asked for, and no more, she ought yet to be satisfied.

Or she ought to ask for more next time.

She shifted to the center of the bench and spread her fingers lightly over the keys. From the stringed heart of the pianoforte, music sounded quiet and sweet.

I sowed the seeds of love …

Chapter Four

Thump. Thump. Thump thump thump thump thump.

Stripped to his shirt-sleeves, Nicholas hit the sandbag again and again. One punch for each day that had passed since he'd fallen asleep to the sound of Ellie playing the pianoforte. One for each night in which he'd slept raggedly again.

For each day he had called on her, only to learn that Barberry had denuded another hothouse in her service.

For each posy he'd sent to Miss Lewis, for each awkward fifteen minutes spent drinking tea under the watchful eye of her mother as she sat in bashful silence.

And some extra blows, quick-fire and sharp, because hitting a suspended pillar of sand wasn't erasing the confusing twists of the past week. Everything was going just as it ought, yet it all seemed *wrong.* He couldn't stop striking until it seemed right again, or until he was too tired to care.

"May I join you, Your Grace?"

Nicholas halted, fists raised and perspiration trickling down his temple, and looked to his side. Lord Killian, an older earl from Ireland who was newly appointed to the House of Lords, was strapping mufflers of wool and leather over his knuckles.

Nicholas caught his breath before answering. "Do you want to box?" He looked at his fists. The bare knuckles were already reddened by the coarse canvas of the sandbag.

"Oh, no, though I thank you. Beating the stuffing out of this bag is sufficient for me." He stood little more than a foot from Nicholas, adopting the boxing stance: light on the balls of his feet, fists at the ready. With his graying dark hair and impeccable form, he could have been the father of

Gentleman Jackson, in whose saloon they now stood.

"I prefer that too." When the sandbag swung toward Nicholas, he hit it with a quick flurry of jabs that sent it swinging toward Killian. "I don't come here to fight; I'm here to become stronger."

Jackson's saloon was tonnish, and some men paid their dues only for the novelty of standing in a ring with the former champion. Plenty of others came to test their own merits and learn from the ever-patient and cordial Jackson.

They boxed in a dim space with gray walls and high-set windows, a smooth wide-planked wooden floor, and a square-off space for formal fisticuffs. To one side of the room was a scale, with a seat on one side and racks of lead weights to counter. The smells of perspiration and liniment, of wet wool and old metal, pervaded the space.

John Jackson was inevitably present, making a circuit of the area whenever he was not occupied in a private match. He drew up now. "My lord. Your Grace. May

I string up another sandbag so you each have your own?"

Nicholas and Killian paused. Met eyes. Said at once, "No, but thank you."

Jackson was a dark-haired man of the duke's age, with a strong-boned face and ears like jug handles. Just under six feet tall, he was solid as a stump. Nicholas had boxed with the champion once and had earned himself bruises and a pair of ringing ears. For each blow he absorbed, Jackson countered with enormous force. A man might put all his effort into a head-long rush and still be halted by a single fist.

"Very well," said the boxer. "No hitting that bag below the belt, now. Use the Broughton rules." He winked. "Your Grace, would you care to wrap your knuckles?"

"Not today." Nicholas rotated his fists, loosening his wrists. "I don't want to soften the blow today."

When Jackson moved along to check the settings on the scale—two men were trying to weigh themselves at the same time—Lord Killian regarded his wrapped hands. "A man who works to become stronger has a better chance of winning should he have to fight in future. But only if he does not fight when he need not."

"No doubt." Not really listening, Nicholas aimed a blow at the sandbag, then followed with a flurry of strikes. Punching from the shoulder, as Jackson taught, holding the rest of himself still.

"Your Grace?" Killian put a flat palm out, halting the sway of the sandbag. "I am being figurative."

"Hmm?" With a forearm, Nicholas shoved back his hair and rubbed perspiration away. The room was warm. His thin linen shirt was sticking to his skin. "Figurative?" What was the man getting at? Here he was, peacefully punching this sandbag, so to speak. Hardly looking for advice.

The older man began easing the wrappings from his fists. "You could do much, Your Grace, with the respect others lend you."

Nicholas bristled. "I have always—"

"But you fight more than you realize. Is insulting a well-meaning widow in her own home a worthy battle?"

Thump. He smashed his fist hard into the sandbag, sending it careening in a crazy direction. "You refer to Lady Frederick, I suppose?"

Killian unwound and re-rolled his mufflers with great concentration, ignoring the sway of the weighted bag inches from his face. "I was in attendance at her recent card party. Her ladyship is not the silent sort."

Nicholas set his jaw. "I merely reminded her that Catholics continue to be excluded from Parliament—an issue over which England lost the best prime minister it ever had."

"I have enormous respect for Pitt," Killian replied, "but he couldn't convince the king to accept Catholics. So Pitt resigned on principle, and now Addington leads. Was that right?"

"For him to resign on principle?" Nicholas let the bag swing back toward him without hitting it. "I believe so.

Though the question is a valid one." Over a matter of principle, the Whig prime minister stepped down—thus handing a seat of power to the other party.

They lost more than they gained. Principle was well and good, but one couldn't effect change from the outside.

Killian's question about Lady Frederick was valid too. She was on the outside, more voiceless as a woman than even Ireland's Catholic lords. Nicholas was a duke, and he could do whatever he damned well wanted to—but he had a conscience, and what he'd wanted to do then, scoring a point off his hostess when he was in a sour mood, hadn't been right.

Maybe that was part of what had felt wrong about this week too.

"You are most illuminating, Lord Killian." Nicholas rubbed the sore knuckles of his right hand.

The Irishman's square face broke into a smile. "Am I? All I did was hit a sandbag."

Nicholas inclined his head. "May we meet over an obliging sandbag again, my lord."

"I am sure we will, Your Grace. And I shall see you in Parliament on Monday."

Two days away. The time seemed long.

A week ago he had slept well, on that narrow sofa in the front parlor of his mother's house, as Ellie's playing lullabied him. Now he had too many thoughts; his head was in a clamor. Punching a bag of sand was good for the muscles of his arms, but it had little other effect.

Maybe Ellie would play for him again. Oh—no, they were supposed to attend a ball together tonight. He'd promised Miss Lewis the first dance.

The music in a ballroom was never as pleasant as that of a pianoforte played by a friend.

Bidding Jackson a farewell, he exchanged the light-soled shoes used in the saloon for his usual top boots, then reassembled his clothing. Back to Hampshire House for a bath, a few hours of working at correspondence and legislation, then he would retrieve Ellie in his carriage.

What would she think of his swollen knuckles? Of his sleeplessness, if she knew of it?

Whatever she thought, she would tell him. And she wouldn't let him slip away from the conversation. She'd look at him with that "you are uttering foolishness" gaze of hers. He had twitted her about it, but it was one of his favorite expressions on one of his favorite faces in the world. It was so damned honest.

As he pushed open the door and stepped out into the afternoon sunlight on Bond Street, he decided: he was going to ice his knuckles once home.

But before then, he had a few flowers to purchase.

Everything Eleanor had packed at Athelney Place was now flung about her bedchamber in the Duchess of Hampshire's house. The red silk bedcovers were hidden under gowns. The large, expensive carpet was patterned with shoes. The bed's heavy gold draperies, hanging from the tester, had been bunched and shoved back, and the similarly gold-upholstered wing chair before the fireplace was bedecked with shawls and stockings.

Sarah Darling, Eleanor's lady's maid, stood amidst the chaos with hands on her hips. "It's no good," she proclaimed. "None of it."

"The gold shawl from Sidney is quite nice." Snatching it up from the tall back of the chair, Eleanor clutched it close.

"Oh, all right." Sarah, a few years Ellie's junior, had a stubborn chin and equally stubborn ideas about how her ladyship ought to be dressed. "Since it's not black or gray, it'll do."

So much of her clothing *was* black and gray, though.

With one of those grand balls in which the *ton* delighted only a few hours ahead, Eleanor was taking a determined inventory of her possessions. Each one represented an investment—of money, of attention, of the modiste's time.

When Palmer ran through her dowry within the first year of their marriage, Eleanor had stopped discarding anything.

Every penny must be pinched until it squealed, every item used and turned and used yet more.

The more careful she became, the more Palmer had laughed and teased her—and gone on spending. Not on things that could have made their lives easier, such as wages for another housemaid, or bespoke boots that didn't pinch Eleanor's toes. No, it went to wagers on games of chance, and gold snuffboxes, and the sort of fashionable nonsense that made a good show to others.

The employment of Sarah had been just such a good-show gesture, or so Palmer regarded it. A lady, he thought, ought to have a lady's maid. But Sarah was far more than that; she was a support and voice of reason as Eleanor's husband became increasingly erratic. With Sarah's help, Eleanor could make a decent show with last year's gowns and bonnets, turned and retrimmed, and turned again the following year. No one needed to know, save the two of them, how difficult things had become.

When Palmer died, his debts fell to his nearest male relatives, and Eleanor had no more tie to them. But she had little else, either. Sidney and Mariah gave her house-room, but she was too proud at the time to ask for more than that. So the twice-turned gowns were dyed inky black. After a year's mourning, they had faded. Some were dyed again in grays and lavenders—wan colors for a widow's half-lived life.

That wasn't the sort of life she wanted.

Why had she kept all her worn-out, unwanted things since Palmer's death? Lack of trust, maybe, that she wouldn't become impoverished again. The fear seemed ludicrous, now that she stood at the center of a duchess's bedchamber, with silk-covered walls and gilt and crystal all about.

She could always have come here, could she not? She could have always asked Sidney for help, or Nicholas. But they hadn't wanted her to marry Palmer—*he's not good enough for you*, they had said—and she would have choked to death on her pride rather than swallow it. Much good had that done her.

Much good was any of this now. She didn't want to wear them, these blacks and grays, the lavender of half-mourning. The secondhand slippers that had never quite fit right. The ones that had, that she'd worn until the soles were thinned to nothing.

"You are right, Sarah," she decided. "Not much of this can be saved. Though the blue gown is all right, and the drab will do for day."

"Only until you can have more clothing made." Sarah folded her arms.

Eleanor wasn't going to argue with that. Who would want to spend her life wearing a color called *drab*?

She set aside the pieces she wanted—or couldn't afford to dispose of yet. The plain shifts, the coarse stockings. More happily, there was the gold shawl and the other one Nicholas had folded, still in its tidy triangle. The blue gown she had worn to Lady Frederick's house. It was plain, but she had felt pretty in it.

"Sarah, I won't keep the rest of this. Have what you like of it, then take the remainder to a used-clothing shop."

She was not going to hold on to her life with Palmer anymore, in any way.

But what would she wear to the ball at Devonshire House that night? Like the ash-covered *Cendrillon* of the old French tale, she owned nothing suitable. She would need the intercession of a wise fairy or a magical dove. Or a sister-in-law.

Clearly, it was time to call on Mariah.

"You would look beautiful in the black and white one, I think." From her bed, the young marchioness regarded the two gowns Eleanor held up. "The fabric is so light, you'll feel like you're floating when you dance."

The gown was elegant, undeniably, of petal-delicate layers of white edged in thick, stark black ribbon. But. "I would rather wear something more colorful," she told her sister-in-law.

"Then you'd best go with the darker purple, though it's not quite as formal. If you bind up your hair in golden fillets, though—oh, Sarah could work a wonder with that." Mariah adjusted the posture of the sleeping baby in her arms, a considering expression on her pleasant face. "She'll have to baste the seams too, or the bodice will be loose on you."

This was true. Mariah was a little taller than Eleanor and sweetly plump. "Sarah is quick as a piston when she bastes. It will be fine. Really, I can't thank you enough for lending me your pretty things."

"All in the name of family goodwill." Mariah grinned. "And romance, perhaps?"

Eleanor had known Mariah before Sidney had. Seven years younger than she—a scant twenty-three—Mariah was the only child of wealthy and ambitious parents. By the time she made her debut, Eleanor was clinging to the edges of the *ton*, respectable but with pockets entirely to let. At those edges, the long-suffering wife and the cit's daughter had met. It had been friendship at first sight.

When Sidney met Mariah and encountered her ever-ready smile, he fell in deep and delighted love. Now, four years after their marriage, they had a lovely little nocturnal son.

"Let me borrow Siddy from you." Eleanor laid the two gowns at the foot of the bed, then made a gentle cradle of her arms for the sleeping baby. "How are you feeling, Mariah? Ready to be up and about?"

The younger woman stretched her arms, rolling her wrists in a circle. "Oof, he's getting heavy, isn't he? Yes, I'm ready to be up. Three weeks of beef tea and novels have me set for months to come. I'm craving archery and a long walk through Hyde Park."

Eleanor held one hand beneath the baby's bottom, one hand at his back. This let his little head nestle into the curve of her shoulder. She inhaled the scent of him: clean cloth, a milky mouth, and the addictive warm scent of new-baby skin. "I'll stay with him. Go shoot a target full of arrows."

Mariah laughed. "As if your brother hasn't engaged the city's finest nurse and nanny to watch over the baby in our absence?"

"Of course he has. Sidney has never been one to settle for a single plan when two or three, all implemented at once, would do as well." Cautious and caring, that was her brother.

It was too easy for her voice to take on an envious edge, and she snuggled the baby more tightly to settle herself. Palmer had never planned anything; he had blamed Eleanor for their childlessness. He probably wouldn't have been a caring father, but he would have been an entertaining one.

Ah, well. She could plan as well as her brother could. As Mariah swung her feet over the edge of the bed and padded about the room in a dressing robe, collecting accessories and jewelry, Eleanor described the progress of her courtship—if it was a courtship?—with Lord Barberry.

Mariah held up a garnet earbob, considering, then returned it to her jewel box. "If you've seen him every day, then it sounds like a courtship to me."

"I've seen Nicholas every day too." Her cheeks heated, but Mariah didn't appear to notice.

"Yes, well, he's part of the family. That's to be expected, isn't it?"

Yes, yes, it was to be expected. Eleanor was being silly. "I could probably convince Lord Barberry to love me, if I bent my efforts and will to the matter. But could I do the same for him?"

"You'll never know unless you pursue the matter." Turning to face Eleanor, Mariah held up two fans. "Do you like the one of carved ebony, or the one with the painting?"

"Ebony, I think." Eleanor crossed to her to eye the delicate fan more closely. "He always asks about my new pianoforte when I see him."

"Lord Barberry?" Mariah's brow puckered. "Oh, no—you mean Nicholas!" She grinned. "What a good gift that was. And how sly you were! All the time you were living here, you never touched the pianoforte. I didn't even realize you were musical."

"It wasn't mine to play." How could she explain to Mariah? Her own instrument had been sold by Palmer, so she oughtn't to get too attached to anyone else's. After all, she had married Palmer against Sidney's advice, against Nicholas's. Had she the right to feel joy?

And yet...a sensible life did not have to be a joyless one. She must remember that. If not playing the pianoforte had been a penance, then surely a benediction had arrived in the form of a wood and string and ivory creation by John Broadwood.

Nicholas had wanted her to have a gift she adored. That was the word he had used: *adore*.

Nestled against her shoulder, the sleeping viscount wiggled his peach-fuzz head.

"You seem," said Mariah, "to enjoy talking about the pianoforte rather more than you like talking about Lord Barberry."

"Only one of them is entirely mine at this point in time," Eleanor quipped.

Without waking, the baby let out a surprising burst of flatulence.

Her sister-in-law smiled, but there was a knowing look in her eye. "Paste jewelry won't do for tonight, if you intend to take possession of someone. We shall have to get out the jewel case."

She was resplendent. Not that Nicholas could tell her that.

"You look very nice, Ellie."

In the dim light that remained at the end of sunset, he could read her wry expression. "Are you certain of that? Doesn't my hair look strange?"

"Since you mentioned it, no, it does not." It was bound up in some sort of Grecian-looking pile, banded with gold ribbons that allowed curls to twine around her face and spill onto her neck. "You look very Ellie-ish, and very nice. May I hand you down?"

They had arrived at Devonshire House, and a servant had opened the door of Nicholas's carriage. He dismounted, cursing the slick soles of his formal dancing shoes, then helped Ellie to clamber down as well. Her gold heeled slippers looked precarious on the steps, but she collected her trailing skirts and hopped to the ground without mishap.

Nicholas retrieved his assortment of flowers, then bade the carriage leave them. He offered Ellie an arm, and together they approached the endless steps upward to the grand entrance of the mansion. Torches split the falling twilight; light poured from the windows of the main floor.

Like Hampshire House, Devonshire House was a palace in all but name. Flat and plain on the outside, inside it was a glittering show of gilt and crystal, of candles and marble. But to reach that, one had to mount two stories' worth of steep stone steps, which were wet from recent rain.

"You look like a hothouse," Ellie observed as they climbed, following a group of richly dressed nobles. "What do you intend to do with all those flowers? Please don't think I'm angling for one. I'm only curious."

He paused, one foot raised to the next step, and drew a posy of red roses from the mass in his arms. "Here, you must take these. The smell of all these flowers together is going to make me faint."

"Ah, so I'm taking them as a good deed?" Her eyes crinkled at the corners.

"That, and I know you like them. I wanted to give you something you would like."

She took the roses in her satin-gloved hand, brow puckered. "As if a pianoforte is not enough?"

"But it's not, is it? If it were all you wanted in this world, you'd be happier."

"I'm..." *Perfectly happy*, he could almost hear her say, but she closed off the sentence. "The pink rosebuds must be for Miss Lewis?"

"Horribly uncreative of me. I got the idea from Lord Barberry."

Her mouth pursed with humor. "And who are the white tulips for?"

The flower of forgiveness—and not a commonly cultivated color. He had paid a small fortune for them. "Lady Frederick, if she'll accept them. I was a bit of a boor at her house."

"She will accept them." Ellie took up her train in her free hand and mounted another step. "People will take anything from a duke."

He hastened to catch up. "I don't want her to take them only because she feels *obligated*."

"Sorry, I don't know how to help you with that. You love flinging your title around, so no one can forget about it."

She sounded annoyed. But why? "Ellie. Wait."

She halted, one step above him, and turned. The line of her neck was strikingly graceful.

"Ellie." He fumbled for words. "I do ... do what I wish, usually. But I greatly value the times when you tell me what I wish is stupid."

For a moment, she was silent—then she laughed, her face a sunbeam backed by the purple of nightfall. "I shall happily tell you that anytime the occasion arises, Nicholas."

"Why do you always call me Nicholas?" he asked.

She smiled. "Sometimes I call you 'Your Grace.'"

He climbed a step to stand at her side. "No, I mean—your brother always calls me Nick, and he and I always call you Ellie. But you call me Nicholas."

"Oh." She looked abashed. With her gloved fingertips, she touched her lips. "It started when we were much younger. I didn't want to call you the same thing Sidney called you. Because I didn't want you to see me the same way."

"How so?"

"As only a friend." She wasn't quite looking at him. "It was...girlish infatuation."

His heart gave a surprised leap. It had been lazy and complacent; now it was paying attention. "Only girlish?"

She ascended one step, her eye level at his. "What do you want...Your Grace? Do you want me to call you Nick?"

Why had he such a cursed big armful of flowers? He couldn't see her as well as he wished. *I want to know how long you were infatuated with me. Or if infatuation was all it ever was.*

"No," he said instead. "I want you to call me whatever seems right to you."

"That depends on the occasion," she said dryly.

"So...why did you call your husband Palmer? Why didn't you call him Adrian? Didn't you want him to see you differently?"

"I didn't worry about that. He was my husband; that made him different from all others." She waved her roses, dividing that sentence from the next. "And being called Palmer was what he liked."

"What did you want to call him?"

"I never thought about that."

He wasn't sure if she was telling him the truth, but he liked the answer anyway.

She was wearing a simple gown tonight, but it was a color. Not a mourning gown; this one was deep, drenched, vivid even in the low light. The color of wine on a just-kissed mouth. Her eyes were curious and liquid.

They were beautiful eyes. He had been looking into them all his life, always sure they would reflect the truth.

Before he thought, before he considered, he climbed to the step on which she stood. Arms full of flowers that were drowsy-sweet and lush, he closed the distance between their faces ... and kissed her.

He didn't know why he had; he knew only that he had wished to. That not to kiss her right now, gold and wine-dark in the moonlight, seemed impossible.

Under his lips, hers opened to match his, a warm welcoming brush of mouth to mouth. He sank into the pleasure of it, tasting her. She hummed, a little sound of deliciousness, and he sipped at it. Oh, she was everything familiar and lovely and right and ...

... and good God, he was kissing *Ellie*. The lips that he'd seen every day for years were pressed against his, opened to him with the passion of a lover.

It was as startling as a bolt of lightning in the night. It was beautiful.

He could have kissed her until the ball ended, until the torches were doused against the coming of the sun. Each kiss, a sweet discovery of something familiar but never known—

—until she broke free and took a step back. Her breath was shallow; her eyes were wide.

For a long moment, they simply stared at each other. "I..." She was the first to speak, but that was all she said. Neither of them quite knew what to say now that the night had changed color, become warm.

Applause rang upward; hoots shattered the crystal silence that connected them. London's wealthy and powerful were climbing the stairs before them, behind them. Nicholas and Ellie had been seen, of course, kissing out in the open like lovers on a stage.

Yet he wouldn't take it back, not for any amount of fast-traveling gossip. He would not wish undone a rain of kisses like that. "Ellie, I—"

"Don't," she said. "Just...don't, Nicholas. Don't make it into anything more." She turned away, and in another moment, she was fleeing up the stairs.

He wasn't going to let her get away that easily. He set a foot on the next step, ready to dash up after her.

But the step was wet. His shoes were slick. The flowers in his arms blocked his sight.

And instead of climbing toward her steadily, it went entirely wrong, and he toppled backward down the steep steps and everything went night-black.

Chapter Five

He awoke to the heavenly scent of tea. Strong tea, dark and fragrant, with a sugary edge.

"Mmm." Bleary eyes blinked open. The world was too bright; he shut his eyes again. "Who's there? I smell tea. Is it for me? I'd give an absolute fortune for it."

"Don't roll over!" Ellie's voice, quick and sharp. "Careful. You're on the sofa in your mother's parlor."

Squinting, Nicholas shaded his eyes and brought the world into focus. It was indeed his mother's parlor; there stood Ellie's piano at the center of the room.

He was lying on the long sofa, folded and propped up at head and feet by bolsters.

His right ankle was encased in a great deal of batting. As if craving his further notice, it gave an angry throb.

Gingerly lifting his head, he took in the rest of his appearance. Waistcoat and shirt. No cravat, no coat. Breeches. A stocking, at least on the foot he could see. No shoes.

Memory flickered. Stone and nightfall. A clamor of voices around him.

"Damn those shoes," he said. "It was the shoes, wasn't it? The soles were slick as ice. How long have I been unconscious?"

"Not long at all." Ellie bustled closer, kneeling beside him. She held a great earthenware mug and extended it to him. Carefully, he took it from her and sipped.

Ah. Heaven. He hadn't noticed his head was throbbing too, as it always did of a morning, until the bracing tea eased the discomfort. "But it's morning," he said after a few more sips.

"You've been sleeping, not unconscious. You did strike your head, but you returned to your senses almost as soon as

Lord Killian arrested your fall and helped you to sit on the lawn beside the steps."

None of that sounded familiar at all. "That memory has gone begging, but it sounds well enough."

She made some sort of a splutter. "You are lucky you are here and not in your family crypt."

He blinked. "But you just implied I was not—"

"Oh, I don't mean you nearly fell to your death. I mean that I was sorely tempted to murder you."

That did *not* sound well enough. "How dire." He looked into the depths of the mug. "Should I suspect poison?"

"Not today." She brushed a falling curl from her face, then rose. She dragged the piano seat toward the sofa. "We'd better have this out."

"What, you're not going to play for me?"

She fixed him with a dire look. "No, Nicholas. I am not going to play for you."

"I don't understand what's happened." He struggled to sit up straighter without sloshing tea all over. "What do we need to have out? Why do you want to murder me?"

She held up her hand, ticking off reasons on her fingers. "You said you liked being told when you did something stupid. Then you immediately did something stupid again. You kissed me! In public, as if I were a doxy! When both of us are meant to be courting someone else!"

Oh. That. *That*, he remembered. "I am sorry?" He really was *not* stupid, and he could tell that saying anything more would be a match to a spill of oil.

But apparently even this short reply was too much. With a huff, she stood, crossed the room to a writing desk, and took up a pair of shears. Yanking an assortment of pink rosebuds from a vase, she lopped off the ends of their stems, one by one. Little bits of green scattered over the carpet.

"What are you doing?" he finally had to ask.

"Something constructive. I am keeping these flowers in good health by cutting off the old ends of their stems." Fixing him with a sharp glare, she brandished the shears at him. "How *dare* you apologize?"

"But I thought you liked it when I apologize."

"Not merely for the sake of apologizing, to get yourself out of hot water. An apology only has meaning if you're truly contrite."

For kissing Ellie? Beautiful, upset Ellie, with a cloud of curling hair and her hands full of roses?

He wasn't contrite at all—not for kissing her. "I understand. I should not have kissed you in public."

She shot him a sidelong glance. "That's not exactly what I meant."

From his awkward position on the sofa, he managed a shrug. "But why am I here, instead of at my own house?"

She stuffed the roses back into their vase, then crouched to pick up the snipped-off pieces of stem. "You were hurt. You were acting strangely. I was worried, despite my murderous mood. I didn't really think—I just said this address to the coachman."

"I've only injured my ankle. That's not much to be concerned about."

"Your ankle might be broken. Now that you are awake, your mother's frightening butler will summon a doctor to set the bones."

He'd had a broken bone set once before in his life. It had not been a pleasant experience. "I wish that had been done while I was asleep. And how was I acting strangely?"

Crossing to the fireplace, she tossed in the handful of stem ends. "You sat up saying, 'She needs to have the roses!' So someone brought Miss Lewis the pink roses, and you said, 'Not those,' and then you cried like a baby."

His jaw dropped. "I did *not*."

When she turned to face him, she was almost smiling. "Well, maybe not that last part. No, you didn't cry. You got huffy and indignant and wanted to know what had happened to your roses."

"Did I mean the red ones? The ones I gave you?"

"Yes." Ellie set the shears back on the desk, then fussed with the flowers in a different arrangement. More pale-colored blooms; there was not a red rose in sight.

"Where are they?"

She took a deep breath, then brushed her hands off against her skirts. "I didn't keep them, Nicholas. When you fell, I dropped them. Will you quit asking about the damned flowers?"

Bracing himself on one elbow, he set the mug of tea on the carpeted floor. "Eventually, but not yet. Was Miss Lewis very upset?"

"Fortunately for you, Lord Barberry's eldest son was more than glad to partner the lady for the first dance."

Not quite an answer, but it would do. "I am grateful to him. And...are *you* very upset?"

"About the fact that you kissed me in public, with little regard for the fact that I am a respectable widow seeking to become engaged to a man of good character?"

"Er—yes. About that."

She passed by the pianoforte, trailing her fingertips silently over the keys. "Lord Barberry himself is convinced that you, the scandalous Duke of Hampshire, were exercising your will on defenseless, vulnerable me."

Now that hurt more than his ankle. "Good God, Ellie. I would be the worst sort of beast if I—did I really—"

"I kissed you back. I take responsibility for that." She settled back onto the bench seat beside the sofa. "But how will you learn to determine if your behavior is foolish or scandalous, even without trying it out first?"

She asked the question with sincerity, not sarcasm, and so he bit back a quick retort.

The truth was, he didn't want to think about his behavior. He wanted to act, swiftly, constantly. Only if he stayed endlessly in motion could he escape the yawning void that pulled at him, wrecking his sleep with loneliness and what-ifs.

Coincidental, then, that it was her next question. Retrieving the mug of tea from the carpet by her foot, she wrapped her hands around it and asked, "What would you do if you weren't a duke? Would you think about it more, if you could do what *you* want without having it be a *ducal* want?"

"I don't know how to separate the two."

"Would you play the pianoforte?"

"Give me back that mug. You're stealing from an invalid." He took it from her and drained the cooling tea to the dregs. "I might play it, yes. I might play it still. What about you? If you hadn't been Palmer's wife, would you be looking for the security of—how did you put it? A man of good character?" A bitter note sharpened those last few words.

She shifted uneasily.

"Ha. The tables are turned, and she does not like it." He returned the mug to its spot on the floor.

"It is an impossible question." She pleated the drab fabric of her skirts. "If I had not married Palmer, I might have married someone else much like him."

This was not a hypothetical direction in which he wished to wander. He should not have asked the question.

"Our marriage was fine. Mostly. Sort of." She let go of the fabric and smoothed it, leaving no trace of her effort behind. "There was no malice in Palmer. He wasn't careful with money or... well, with anything entrusted to him. He didn't mean harm. He simply didn't think about consequences or the future."

Indeed. Well, she might have accused Nicholas of the former, but no one could say he didn't prepare for the future. His correspondence with his steward to care for his tenants, the relationships he sought to build in Parliament, the damned *wife* he was supposed to be finding—all were for the sake of others, and of those who would come after.

"Palmer wasn't good enough for you," Nicholas said.

Green eyes met his. "Oh, nonsense, Nicholas. You've always said that about any man who showed the slightest bit of interest in me. Were the decision up to you, I'd have been a spinster all along."

That didn't sound so bad; they could have gone on as before, in their friendly intimacy, without others coming between them. "Maybe that would have been easier than the difficult years you lived with him. At least you didn't bear his—"

"Don't say it." Eleanor's voice was quick as a whip crack. "Don't say something I won't be able to forgive you for."

He gritted his teeth. His ankle was aching now like the devil. "Ellie...he hurt you. He would have hurt any child of yours too."

"No. Circumstance hurt me. And now you hurt me." She sighed. "Only someone who has never wished to wed or have a child can dismiss the importance of such desires so easily."

She said all of this in a tone as cultured and calm as ever. But in her eyes, a warning green spark shone—and tied his tongue.

"You questioned my judgment when I married him," she said. "I see you are still questioning it now."

Question her judgment? Rubbish. He trusted it more than his own. But resentment burned, and his ankle throbbed, and there were so many pink roses about, and—and once again, he said what perhaps he ought not. What he had never intended to. "I question you, yes. When my father died eight years ago, instead of standing friend to me, you all but eloped with a near stranger."

Her mouth fell open. She rocked back on the seat, eyeing him from a greater distance as though she did not quite recognize him. "You think I ought to have paused my life for your mourning? Have I not mourned enough for your taste?"

Taste. He had a bad taste in his mouth. "I don't want to talk about how you felt after Palmer died. I'm only saying that I thought, as a lifelong friend, that you could have been available to me after I suffered a loss." He sounded stuffy, he knew, but to hell with it. This was something that had long nagged at him, though he had never put words to it before.

She arched a brow. The woman could have posed for a classical statue—the Muse of Skepticism. "Were either you or your mother particularly sorry when he died?"

"Ellie. That's cruel."

"I don't mean to be cruel. I certainly don't mean that you were pleased, for you're not cruel yourself. But you weren't attached to him. He wasn't the sort of person who welcomed family feeling." Drumming her fingers on the satin-smooth wood of the bench, she added, "If you want to talk of unkindness—I think he did you a great one by raising you to think that the world owes you whatever you want."

"Obviously, it doesn't," he grumbled, "because you didn't even come to his funeral. You were being courted instead."

She blew out a breath through thinned lips. "Women never go to funerals, Nicholas. We are too fragile and sentimental to handle the sight of a churchyard, and we might cause a spectacle with our weeping."

Oh. He had forgot that was the tradition. But still, he had some spleen to vent. Elbowing the bolsters and cushions behind him with the same force he'd used on Jackson's sandbag, he hauled himself upright.

But she was talking again. "And anyway, Palmer didn't really start courting me until after the funeral. It was ... swift." She colored.

He forgot the splendid rant he'd begun to formulate. "Why are you blushing?"

She shook her head.

Which made him wonder and imagine. Had Palmer kissed her until her cheeks flushed pink? Had Palmer seen her hair unpinned and riotous before their wedding night? Had he run his fingers through the tangle of curls, loving the feel of coarse silk twining about his knuckles? Or had she made herself sleek for him, as she had become the night she met Lord Barberry, with all her exuberant bits tidied away?

He had been looking at her as he wondered these things, and she had been looking back at him. Though she sat on the bench seat by the sofa, completely separate, he felt as if she had fallen into his embrace. Her eyes were as frank, as lovely, as they had been when he'd had to kiss her.

"I allowed Palmer to court me," she said, "because you had just become the Duke of Hampshire."

"What the devil does that have to do with anything?"

She smiled, but it wasn't happy. "Just this: I had waited for three Seasons for you to notice that we had grown up and that I was a woman as well as your old friend. But if you never noticed me when you were a carefree marquess, what hope did I have of catching your notice once you were a duke?"

She spoke in a clear, quiet voice, but he was not sure he had understood her correctly. Her words were sounds, clanging on resistant eardrums, for it was impossible that she had said what he thought she had.

"Are you saying"—it was difficult to look her in the eye, but he made himself do it—"that you married Adrian Palmer because of me?"

"Indeed not. I married him for myself. Because I wanted to marry and have a family and home of my own. And since you'd refused to fall in love with me, or even make a dutiful offer for my hand, I took up with the most entertaining man I'd ever met."

The words caused a pain that was almost physical, and he sucked in air, hard, to keep his breath. "Ouch. That hurt."

"You haven't the right to be hurt. I chose Palmer because I thought he would help me forget about you. And it worked for a while. He spent a lifetime's worth of money in a year, and then we were deep in debt." She laced her fingers together in her lap, studying them. "Debt is very preoccupying, or at least it was for me."

"Hold on. Wait." He was still trying to let her words in, still trying to have his muddled brain make sense of them. "I was the one you wanted?" Lightness blazed through him, a sudden surprised joy.

She leaned forward, her chin propped on her hands. "You were, yes. I knew few other people, and we had always enjoyed each other's company. It was natural, I think, that I should become besotted with you."

"You don't flatter me with that statement."

"Ah, well." Unfolding to her feet, she stepped back to the pianoforte. A sheaf of music was centered on the stand. "Even dukes must hear a thing or two they don't adore sometimes."

He cursed his ankle to hell and beyond. If he could just stand—well, maybe he could. He swung his good leg to the floor.

"Don't," she said, "even think about putting any weight on that ankle."

"Too late," he grunted, dragging his leg back up onto the sofa. He was thinking about it plenty, putting weight on his injured ankle. About following her across the room and taking one hand in his. Dropping to his knees, begging her, *Wait, please, tell me the truth. All of it. I never knew any of this; I never knew how you felt.*

It was too late to say that, and the bubble of elation within him popped. He was hollow inside, just as his sleepless nights always confirmed. "So you don't care for me anymore."

"Of course I care for you." She shuffled through the music sheets.

"But not like that."

She took a moment to square the printed music into a neat pile, then set it aside. When she turned toward him, the movement was as deliberate as that of a clockwork figure. "Nicholas, what are you getting at? Do you want me to tell you that I've loved you and only you all my life? Do you want me to say I've been waiting for you, and no one else will do? Do you want me to drop to one knee and beg you to marry me?"

"No. Of course not." Though the thunder of his heart gave the lie to his words.

"Right. Because you know those things are impossible. You and I want different things out of marriage, and that's quite all right." With the thumb of her right hand, she rubbed the spot where a ring would be. "And we've both found people who will be what we want—if, that is, you can pry Miss Lewis from the arms of Lord Barberry's son. Likely you and I will both wed, and we'll continue being friends, and you'll continue being a duke and having everything the way you like it."

In what she said, there was nothing that he liked. "You don't love me anymore."

She rubbed her temples. "Of course I love you."

"But not like *that*," he finished with bitter triumph.

"You don't really want to know the answers, Nicholas. You only want to ask the questions."

"I bloody well do want answers!"

She winced.

"Sorry," he muttered. "That was coarse." His ankle had better not be seriously injured. One morning on a sofa and he was ready to run mad.

"An apology. Good for you." Now that she'd finished with the sheet music, she seemed to be looking for something else to fidget with.

"Ellie. Tell me the truth. What do you really want?"

She seized upon a triangle of cloth that had been laid inside the heart of the pianoforte. "The truth is, you're lucky I haven't any more laudanum, or I'd have doped you into silence. The truth is that you think your words are gold. That I should always listen and you should always get what you want."

"Uh. That's not the sort of truth I wanted."

She looked almost wistful. "That makes one thing that you got that you didn't want, then. Too bad. If you ask me for truth, you're going to get it."

Yes. That was the way it had always been with Ellie. There was an odd sort of comfort in the way she harangued him. "I didn't think," he said. "I'm sorry."

"I know you didn't." Taking hold of the edge of the cloth, she shook it out in one quick snap. "You didn't mean it that way. You didn't think about how it would sound. You didn't consider what you were asking of me, or implying.

"You didn't think of what it would mean to me, to have you kiss me on the steps of Devonshire House. You didn't think of how it would look to everyone who saw it, to have you treat me so lightly, or how Lord Barberry would react. You just…do things, dragging tiny scandals in your wake. And it's the people left behind who are shaken. For you, it's all smooth sailing."

The cloth, he now saw, was a shawl. He had folded a shawl much like that once, hadn't he? "What do you want me to do about it? How can I fix matters for you?" Never had he come so close to pleading.

"You need not. I'll find the answers myself." Taking up the shawl, she wrapped it around her shoulders like armor. "Nicholas, I want to be loved. I don't think there could ever be too many people in the world who love me. Certainly there are not too many now."

That did not follow at all. "If you want to be loved, you're not going about this husband hunt the right way. You're look-ing at sticks who don't even have hearts."

"First they were prigs, now they are sticks. Whatever you want to call them, they're the sort of man who won't kiss me in public without asking for my hand first. They're the sort who don't take the esteem of others for granted. The sort I can respect."

Men, in other words, nothing like him. And did that mean she didn't respect him?

He couldn't ask her right now. He suspected he would not like the answer.

Pushing a hairpin into a rogue curl of hair, she said, "Since you're here until your ankle can be set, I'm returning to Sidney's house. Though soon you'll not have to worry about me at all. If Lord Barberry asks me to marry him, I'll say yes."

Chapter Six

"I have brought you pink roses, Lady Eleanor," said Lord Barberry. "Your favorite."

He had called upon her just as she was preparing to leave the house—not for an afternoon walk, but for good. Her remaining garments were packed away; Sidney's carriage awaited, ready to take her and her belongings back to Athelney Place.

And now, pink roses, again. No one would give her what she wanted if she didn't ask. She knew that.

Though she had never dreamed of asking for a pianoforte.

"Thank you, Lord Barberry. They are lovely." She breathed in their insipid scent, forcing a smile. "Though I admit, my favorite roses are red ones. Great large ones."

"Oh." He looked taken aback. "You don't find them vulgar?"

"It seems not." Eleanor glanced at the closed door across the corridor, behind which a doctor was examining Nicholas's ankle. It seemed improper for Lord Barberry to call here while Nicholas was here as well. Undecided, she toyed with the lapel of her gray spencer.

"Would you care to accompany me for a walk?" she finally asked. "The day is so fine."

In truth, the weather was undecided too. Today had included everything from sunshine to mizzle, and just now clouds turned the sky a pewter shade that belied the early hour.

"Of course I will walk with you." Barberry held the sheaf of pink roses toward Eleanor. "Would you care to bring these along?"

"Let us have a servant put them in a vase," she suggested. A vase that would stay here in the dowager duchess's house, but she didn't have particular regret over that.

Once the roses were dispensed with, Eleanor tied on a hat. It was a jaunty one that she liked, a soft hat of straw that tipped over her right ear and framed her face. A wide dove-gray ribbon tied beneath her chin to keep it fast.

When she turned toward Lord Barberry, expecting him to offer her an arm, he instead paused. Hesitated—and then, with gentle fingers, he tucked a lock of hair under her hat. "You wouldn't want to look untidy when we walk out."

Her hand lifted to touch the lock he'd hidden away. "Oh. Thank you." The urge to pull it down and shake out her hair in a long curly tumble seized her for a moment, but she only smiled politely and preceded him out the door.

Hanover Square offered a fine space for walking, with modern pavements before the houses and a great grassy space in the center of the square. Walking paths crossed it vertically, horizontally, and diagonally, creating a pattern Eleanor now realized was like the new Union flag.

Which made her think of Lady Frederick's ballroom. Which made her think of Nicholas.

She shivered, buttoning the short front of her spencer.

"Are you cold?" Lord Barberry was solicitous as he walked beside her. With each step, he planted a walking cane with a crunch of wood and stone that was not unpleasant.

"No, not at all. A goose walked over my grave—isn't that the old saying?"

"A superstition." He smiled kindly. In the gentle daylight, his hair shone the same pewter as the sky, and lines were visible at the corners of his eyes. "If you would permit the liberty, there is something particular I should like to discuss with you."

Here it came: the proposal for which she had been angling, from a thoughtful and sensible man. She swallowed. "Of course."

They took a few more steps along the graveled path before he spoke again.

"I never thought," he began, "to marry again, since my children are grown. But since meeting you, the idea has taken root. Like a rosebush."

"Oh," she said. "Yes?" Some form of encouragement was required.

"Your companionship is everything proper and pleasant."

A surprised laugh burst from Eleanor's throat.

"What have I said?" His lordship looked bewildered.

"My brother would disagree with your statement. The thought struck me as humorous."

"Ah, I see. Siblings. Most amusing. My sons enjoyed teasing each other when they were young, I remember."

And they didn't anymore? What kind of brothers *were* they? "I didn't mean to interrupt," Eleanor said demurely. "Please, go on. You were saying?"

"Yes, yes. Your companionship." They reached the intersection of two paths, and he looked at her with raised brows. "This way?"

"If you wish." A damp breeze tickled her cheeks and tugged free a lock of hair from under her hat. Before Barberry could reach for it, she tucked it away again. He looked pleased.

"I do not require a dowry," said Barberry, "as my financial situation is sound. With investments in the funds, we may rely on a steady income at a dependable rate of return. And if children should grace the household in future, they would be most welcome."

"That all sounds sensible," she said.

He halted under a tree. Its shading leaves speckled his face with light and shadow, and it was difficult to read his expression. "Does that mean you will do me the honor of accepting my hand?"

He extended one gloved hand to her. It was a fine glove of dyed kidskin, the same gray shade as her old half-mourning pelisse.

She had married for adventure once, and her choice had been poor. Yes, Palmer had twirled her about a ballroom as if they were the only two in the world. He had sneaked into a garden to pick roses for her by the light of the full moon. He had whipped them off to the seaside at a moment's notice.

But he had never cared for the consequences of his impulse. The spending, the spectacle, the inconvenience. And there were always consequences, and they always fell to Eleanor to tidy up.

Barberry was a sensible choice. She did not love him, but she could become fond of him. He would not waste money or flaunt a mistress. Perhaps he would not even stray. And wasn't that all worth something? Wasn't security, when one totted up all its advantages, close enough to love?

She ought to be ecstatic. Delighted. Instead, she felt...sort of pewter inside. A little gray, not as shiny or precious as she'd hoped.

"I accept." She placed her hand in his and tried to feel as if she'd done the right thing.

It was just like any other early afternoon in the study of Hampshire House, except for the footstool on which Nicholas had propped his bandaged right foot. The physician had dubbed the injury a sprain rather than a fracture, and the ankle was immobilized in a length of cotton bandage that crossed over and around his arch.

With his bare toes visible, he felt oddly vulnerable.

But! He had plenty to do now that he was back at home, with crutches to master and a desk full of papers to review. Any time. Right now. The sooner, the better. He had a platter of sandwiches at hand, and tea, and a full inkpot and fresh quills.

When his butler announced Lord Athelney, Nicholas welcomed the visitor at once.

"Sid, do you care for a..." He looked around the room. Surrounded by bookshelves and priceless oils and cluttered with papers, the study was a cozy, chaotic space. "I'm not certain what I have to offer you, but there ought to be a decanter on the sideboard over there. Or here, I have a few sandwiches left on this plate. The cook made them an hour ago. Beef and onion."

Sidney flung himself into a chair across from Nicholas's desk. "In a minute. I bring you news."

Nicholas had missed yesterday's session of Parliament, thanks to his cursed ankle. "Oh? Has Addington resigned?"

"A vain hope. No, this is a personal matter. Ellie is betrothed."

Nicholas sat up straight. His right foot thumped to the floor, making him wince. "Impossible." *Not impossible.* She'd told him she planned to accept Barberry, but somehow he hadn't, well, accepted that.

"The happy couple"—Sidney's tone was dry—"told me the news themselves. Barberry asked her yesterday."

Nothing was any good then. The tea tasted like dirty water, the sandwiches were dust. The study was not cozy but dim and oppressive.

"Hand me a glass from the sideboard, if you please," he said to Sidney.

The marquess looked a question at him, but unfolded from the chair and retrieved a glass from its home behind a pile of books on the sideboard. He set it on the desk before Nicholas, atop a pile of papers, and resumed his seat.

Nicholas picked up the glass. It was crystal, probably. Heavy and fine, catching the light from the tall west-facing windows.

Hefting it in one hand, he threw it at the marble fireplace, shattering it against the stone.

At the sound of something valuable being utterly destroyed, he felt a tiny bit better.

"Unusual display of temper for you." Sidney looked unperturbed.

"The mess is regrettable, certainly." Gritting his teeth, Nicholas hauled his injured limb back into place, propped on the footstool.

"What's the reason for the rotten mood?"

"I can't get around. I'm bored. I've nothing to do."

Wordlessly, Sidney eyed the newspapers and correspondence spilling in untidy stacks across the desk. The shelves and shelves of much-consulted books. The deck of cards scattered on the floor, where it had fallen when Nicholas had bumped it with an elbow.

"Get the damned decanter." Nicholas swiped his hand across the desk to clear a spot at the center. Obliging, Sidney clunked a decanter and two glasses in the eye of the paper storm.

The marquess unstoppered the decanter and took a whiff. "Buttery. Sharp. That's quite nice. Is it a Scotch whisky?"

"Yes, and a very good one."

Sidney poured a measure into each of the two glasses. "Don't throw yours until you drink that down."

"Ha." In one quick motion, Nicholas tossed the whisky back. It burned his palate, his throat, all the way down through his chest.

"I say this to you as an old friend who has only your best interests at heart." Before reseating himself, Sidney picked up a shard of the glass from the hearth. "You look like hell."

Nicholas rubbed a hand over his chin. He needed a shave.

"Not just because you're as stubbled as a field after harvest."

"You've been waiting for an opportunity to use that wordplay, haven't you?"

"I have. I really have. It was clever of me." Sidney held the broken crystal up to catch the cool afternoon light. "Having trouble sleeping again?"

He was one of the few people who knew about the insomnia. Even, as Nicholas had described to him in a tired moment, the wall he built of his thoughts, and the claws of worry that constantly scrabbled to bring it down. He was used to outrunning the claws, but now that he couldn't run…damnation, the hours were long.

"There's no 'again' about not sleeping well. It's 'still.'" The only time he'd slept worth a damn lately had been on that hard sofa in his mother's parlor, with Eleanor nearby playing quiet tunes on the pianoforte.

"Is it because of Parliament? I assume you're not attending today's session either, which is just as well. Since Nelson was granted his viscountcy, then sailed off to Russia, each discussion touching on the war threatens to drag on ten times as long."

"I am decidedly not concerned about that."

"Nelson," Sidney continued as if he hadn't heard, "has done a great deal for this country. But so do the people who sew Great Britain and Ireland together in a proper marriage, as you once put it."

"Don't speak of marriage to me right now." Should he have another whisky? Probably not.

He poured out another measure and drank it with the same speed as the first.

Sidney dropped the piece of crystal onto the desk. "Give me that decanter if you're going to gulp fine aged whisky like it's the rawest gin. You're wasting it."

"Maybe for your birthday next year, I'll send you a bottle. Of gin." Nicholas wrapped his hands around the bulbous decanter. "Do you know Lord Killian? He hinted I ought to pick my battles more carefully."

"Hmm."

"Ellie said, though not in quite these words, that I need not be an arse."

Sidney laughed. "I always thought Ellie was the wisest of us. Was she talking about politics?"

"And romance." And then he'd gone and been an arse to Ellie. He had kissed her in public, making her a party to gossip. And she was right, he had questioned her judgment.

Not because he truly thought her choices were wrong. But because they were taking her farther away from him.

Why did Ellie *want* all these things? Why was she so set on a family of her own? Was it because she'd lost her parents when she was a young child?

Was it because she really was wiser than he was?

Because one of the things that kept him up at night was the knowledge that people generally liked him because he was a duke, or sat in the House of Lords, or could provide a courtesan at an hour's notice.

His life was just like this desk: cluttered at the edges and empty at the center.

Except for Ellie and Sidney, who had always been there. True friends, who smiled at him because he was *him*—and glared at him a damned lot too. At the heart of hearts was Eleanor, peacekeeping and dishing out sense, bearing her own losses, generous and kind and fiery and impatient.

Ever since he'd met her, his life hadn't been entirely empty at the center. By God, why hadn't he asked her to take a larger part in it? Why hadn't he *begged* her? There was nothing good without her.

"You look," Sidney said, "as if you want to hit your head on your desk."

On his desk? He wanted to clash it between cymbals. His head was in a clamor, ringing with new questions.

And a single, steady realization.

"I love her." The words, unexpected and quiet, were ... right.

Yes. He loved her. How long had that been the case? When had friendship become more?

Maybe it had always been more. He could not remember a time his day had not become better at the sight of her. And it wasn't the music she'd played that had allowed him to rest. It was her; it was her giving him a makeshift family.

Idly, as if he'd heard nothing of import, Sidney commented, "She's going to a musical performance at Lady Frederick's house tonight."

Nicholas groaned. "Lady Frederick would doubtless prefer I never darken her doorstep again."

"Then I guess you'd better grovel."

"I attempted a grovel recently, though it ended up in the mud outside Devonshire House."

A shame. The white tulips had been pretty, and not inexpensive.

At least he'd managed to give Ellie her red roses, even if she didn't keep them long.

Sidney tilted his glass, setting the liquor into a gentle swirl. "I did mention at one time that I was reluctant to have Eleanor hurt."

"As am I. I always have been."

"Then see to her happiness." Sidney smiled—almost.

"I intend to." His brows knit. "How long have you known?"

"That you love my sister?" Sidney scoffed. "Please. It was obvious to me the first time you looked at her, years on years ago. I am the oldest of the three of us, and clearly I've been the wisest."

"You said only a few minutes ago that Ellie was."

"I take that back. Because the two of you aren't wed, are you? For the second time, she's going to marry the wrong person." Taking a sip of the whisky, Sidney frowned. "Barberry's less wrong than Palmer, and he won't make her unhappy, but…I'm not sure he'll make her happy, either."

Maybe. Maybe not. But if Barberry was who she wanted, if the safe and secure life was where her heart lay, then that was that. It wasn't Nicholas's place to question her judgment again.

But he didn't have to let her go without a word, either.

"Making her happy will be my first priority," he assured Sidney, hoisting himself to his feet. "I have a plan."

After all these years, he would not put himself at its center. He would not leave it puffed up and void within. No, this plan would be for Ellie.

He added, "I'll practice on these crutches so I can be up and about soon. Expect to see me in Parliament for the session...say, Thursday." After tonight's session, that would be the next.

"I'll see you there." Sidney drank off his whisky, then returned the glass to the desk. "But if you're on your feet before then, you ought to come and see the baby. He has started smiling."

"You are a lucky man," he told Sidney.

"Why, by having a family of my own?" His friend stood, ready to depart. "I am indeed. And if you play your cards right, maybe you'll be my brother. Can't get luckier than that."

The daylight was gone, and the lamps were lit in Eleanor's bedchamber. She was nearly ready to leave for the evening's musical performances at Lady Frederick's house. Sitting at her dressing table, facing herself in the glass, she turned her head to poke an earring into the hole in her lobe. She turned the other way. Held up the second crystal drop. Hesitated.

When she put in the second earring, it would be time to go downstairs, to wait for Barberry. He would come for her once Parliament adjourned for the evening.

She was wearing the white and black gown from Mariah that was so severely elegant. Her hair was smooth and restrained, after an ungodly amount of pomade and pins were slicked and poked into it. Barberry would like it that way.

Without consulting a printed peerage, she would never have known his first name: Horace. Barberry was what everyone called him, what he expected her to call him.

Rather like Palmer, that.

If she asked Sarah to turn the lamps down lower, she would hardly have to face herself anymore.

After she'd put her hand in his, she had asked him to kiss her. He had looked startled, unmistakably startled, through the dappled light of the tree. Glancing around to make sure they were unseen, he then obliged with a quick peck on her lips.

"No more of this now," he said. "We mustn't make a spectacle of ourselves."

How much or how little did it take to make a spectacle of oneself? Would she spend every day wondering? Would careful order and good intentions wrap her tight as a winding sheet?

He didn't love her.

She knew he didn't, of course, but she hadn't really thought about what that meant. Palmer had loved her in his way, but he had not respected her. Barberry respected her but didn't love her—and because to be loved was what she wanted, she would soon stop respecting herself.

In the glass, her eyes looked shadowed. Had she not known their color, she would not be able to tell what it was.

Nicholas had been honest with her the day before, as brutally honest as she'd been with him. And he'd been right: she had married Palmer for the wrong reasons.

He was her *instead of*, her distraction. Her hope that they'd both grow together enough to make a marriage work. But they had grown apart, their differences magnified. Her determination, his impulsiveness: they grated wrongly, like chalk and cheese.

With Lord Barberry, she seemed the impulsive one. Too young, too fond of brightness, too eager to laugh.

"Are you ready to go, my lady?" Sarah's voice broke into her reverie.

Was she ready? One more earring, then she could get up, right now, and walk into that life. It would be a safe life, a dependable one. Barberry would give her everything she asked, if he could.

But no more than that. She could not command him to love her. She ought not to expect him to change for her. Only one person had she ever loved, just as he was. Thoughtful and arrogant and well-meaning and imperfect, all the contradictions that made life interesting.

She didn't want only to be married. She wanted to be *loved*. And maybe that wouldn't ever happen, but she wouldn't settle again for a second-best life.

"My lady?" Sarah asked again.

"No. Not yet." Eleanor set down the crystal earring with a satisfying click, then removed its twin. Deliberately, she pulled the pins from her hair and pattered them over the top of the dressing table too.

"Clean the pomade from my hair, please, Sarah, and let it curl. But first, I have to change my gown."

Chapter Seven

Lady Frederick's flag-bedecked ball-room was as suited to an evening of musical performances as it was to a card party—which was to say, not really. But, Nicholas had to admit, it made for a pleasant sight. The long room was filled with rows of small chairs facing the eastern wall of windows. They showed a void and black sky without, but within was a wood floor of golden gloss, footmen carrying trays with flutes of wine, and a makeshift stage with chairs, stringed instruments, and a grand pianoforte.

He did not want to know how, or with what effort, the pianoforte had been hoisted up the house's steps, past the ground floor, and into the ballroom above. Climbing the stairs on his crutches, with nothing to lift but his own cursed weight, had been grueling enough.

Well. Maybe he did want to know how the feat had been managed, at that. Anything to distract him from noticing that Ellie was late. Parliament had adjourned long ago, and everyone else who was expected tonight was here— except for Lady Eleanor Palmer and Lord Barberry.

He didn't want to think about why that might be.

Fortunately, a diversion interrupted his futile wonderings just then. "Your Grace." Lady Frederick stood at his elbow. "My footman said this was from you."

As beplumed and exuberantly dressed as ever, his hostess looked wary as she indicated the wigged servant behind her. With jaw set in an expression of strain, he hoisted a potted tree a yard tall. Its glossy green leaves were bright and toothy. If a plant had an expression, this one wore a grin.

But Nicholas had better not. It was time to grovel. "Lady Frederick, I was ungracious the last time you were so kind as to welcome me into your home, and I apologize for that. Thank you for extending another invitation."

True, Sidney had managed the matter, but Lady Frederick might as well get the credit. As he waited for her reply, Nicholas hitched a crutch more firmly under one arm, drawing attention to his injured ankle. Though he'd stuffed his heavily bound foot into a pump large enough to fit a giant, the crutches gave him the unmistakable air of an invalid who had wanted, tried, determined desperately to be here. If that helped her ladyship forgive his trespasses, it was all to the good.

"Oh. I didn't expect...that is, don't give it another thought, Your Grace." Lady Frederick looked hesitant. "I do not recognize the little tree. Has it some significance?"

"Indeed it does. It's a cane apple— or some might call it an Irish strawberry tree."

The footman holding up the pot grunted. Lady Frederick noticed the alarmingly red cast of the straining man's complexion. "Good heavens, James! Take it to the conservatory and set it down." After he vanished, shuffling awkwardly as he carried the pot, she added, "Irish, you said, Your Grace?"

"It is. It grows only in Ireland but, I hope, will flourish in your conservatory." Nicholas attempted to sketch a bow without losing his balance and falling arse-end up on the floor. "You have welcomed the Irish into our union"—he did not say, *and in a most patronizing way*—"with great enthusiasm, and now you have a little piece of Ireland for your home. In autumn, when it grows larger, it will bloom and grow fruit."

Her ladyship's whippet-thin face softened. "That is most thoughtful of you. I thank you sincerely."

He tried for another bow.

This ought to have concluded the conversation. Indeed, Lady Frederick was already turning away to speak to one of the night's performers, a young woman clutching a violin about its neck.

But he had one more thing to say. "Lady Frederick." Once she turned to face him again, he lowered his voice to a confidential tone. "I am sorry to ask you for a favor, ma'am, but I must impose once more. Might there be time for me to offer a brief performance this evening?"

By the time Eleanor arrived alone, breath-less from her mad dash up the stairs, the musical performances had already begun. Backed by the tall flag-flanked windows of the ballroom, a harpist in a flowing white gown plucked strings while wearing a beatific expression.

Eleanor sidled into the back of the room, not wanting to draw notice from the scores of listeners in their tidy rows of chairs. The day had been longer than long, and she hadn't really wanted to come, but now that she'd changed into her blue gown and her hair was properly a-tumble, she *had* to go out. It was a matter of principle—or maybe of pride in herself.

She hardly listened as the harpist concluded her piece, then stood and bowed to great applause.

A footman passed by Eleanor with a deliberate glance she found rather impudent, then made his way to the side of the low platform on which the instruments had been placed and where Lady Frederick stood. As applause dwindled, he communicated some message to her. The woman nodded, dismissing the servant, and stepped up onto the makeshift stage.

When she lifted her hands, the assembled guests quieted again. "Tonight," she called in a carrying tone, "I am delighted to present a special performance from His Grace, the Duke of Hampshire."

Nicholas? He wasn't musical—at least, not enough to perform in public. What on earth ...? She craned her neck to get a better look at the raised area being used as a stage.

Dutiful applause followed her ladyship's words, combined with carrying whispers of curiosity. They followed Nicholas as he swung and stepped, crutches and sound foot in turn, to the center of the performers' area.

"Thank you, Lady Frederick, and thank you all for your kind welcome." He looked roguish, his clothing rumpled and awry due to the tug the crutches. Short locks of dark hair had shaken over his forehead. Barberry would tidy those back.

"I intend to perform a special piece for you all tonight," he added. "I learned it from a musician who plays from the heart. I was an inept student for many years, and you will doubtless observe shortcomings in the quality of my playing. The blame for that belongs on my shoulders alone."

Another smattering of polite applause as Nicholas turned, leaned his crutches against the side of the pianoforte, and hopped to take a stance before the center of the keyboard.

Eleanor was getting apprehensive about this.

With a great show of preparation, Nicholas limbered his wrists and placed his hands on the keys. And then...with one forefinger, one deliberate note at a time, he picked out a tune.

The notes jangled in Eleanor's ears, meaningless, as she tried to assimilate the sight of the Duke of Hampshire poking his way through a pianoforte tune before scores of mystified nobles. What was he playing at, besides an odd attempt at music? Was he making mock of Lady Frederick again? No, for their hostess stood to one side with a cat-that-ate-the-canary smile, as if this performance was entirely to her liking.

One note at a time, one vibrating string at a time, the song continued—and at last, the muddle resolved into sense. She *knew* this tune. She knew it by heart, for she'd played it for Nicholas.

I sowed the seeds of love,
It was all in the spring...

By the time he concluded his performance, her heart was in a thunder. She lifted her hands to cheeks grown hot—with confusion, with embarrassment, with hope.

Nicholas turned, bowed, and retrieved his crutches in an excruciating silence. Lady Frederick stepped forward, clapping her hands with great enthusiasm.

"Your Grace, thank you! Thank you for a most unique performance!" Her wink at Nicholas could not have been broader. "I fear you need more lessons, though!"

Relieved laughter eddied through the audience, followed by more applause. Under the growing wall of sound, Eleanor could not hear Nicholas's smiling reply, but he soon followed Lady Frederick from the stage. She did not see where he went then, or whether he even remained in the room.

The next performer was a cellist, a man with a grand waxed moustache who took an age to tune his instrument. While he was still fussing with the pegs, a voice at Eleanor's right said, "My lady?"

She stifled a yelp. "Oh! Lady Frederick! My apologies—I was lost in thought."

"I should think so." The older woman smiled. "If you do not mind missing the cellist's performance, His Grace would like to speak with you. There is a private parlor beyond this ballroom; simply retrace your steps and open the next door on the right."

Eleanor searched her hostess's face. "I do not understand."

"It's not for me to explain, my lady."

All right. Fine. Nicholas was up to some devilry, and he had enlisted Lady Frederick as an accomplice. But... it seemed to be *nice* devilry, if strange.

I sowed the seeds of love...

"I do not mind missing the cellist's performance." Eleanor echoed Lady Frederick's words. "Thank you, ma'am."

"Think nothing of it!" Her ladyship leaned in closer to Eleanor's ear, then whispered in a tone of glee, "The Duke of Hampshire apologized to me! Can you credit it?"

His tulips had gone in the mud, and he had tried again. *Well done, Nicholas.* "Actually... I can."

She found the private parlor, just as Lady Frederick had directed, and pushed open the door with hands that trembled.

"Ellie, thank God. I hoped you'd come speak to me." Nicholas had evidently been waiting by the doorway. He shut the door behind her, then paused. "May I lock the door, so we are not interrupted? I ask for only a few minutes of your time."

"Um ... all right. If you like." While he worked the key, she looked around. The small room was cozy and warm and fire-licked. Paper in a light print of gold and gray hung on the walls, and gilt-framed mirrors flung candlelight about the space. It was just the sort of space where she might again pull the pins from her hair, settle into a deep-seated chair, and feel perfectly at home.

But she wasn't home. She didn't even know if she *had* a home. In the last fort-night, she'd lived in too many places and changed too many plans to know any more than which way was up.

And to know too that when Nicholas turned away from the door toward her, she had never before seen the look on his face. It was one of curious intensity, his eyes fixed on hers as though he could imagine looking nowhere else.

He braced himself with a palm against one wall, lifting his injured foot. "You might wonder," he drawled, "what I said to Lady Frederick upon concluding my performance."

"That is not the first question that came to my mind." She motioned for him to hop to a chair near him. "Sit, Nicholas, before you topple over. Then tell me what you said, since you obviously wish to." She sat in another chair facing him, across the fireplace. Like an adversary—or maybe a new audience.

He shifted his weight in the chair, frowning at his bandaged ankle. "This is most annoying."

Eleanor laughed. "You are too hard on yourself. It wasn't a typical performance, but I was not annoyed by it."

"Ha. I mean that having a sprained ankle is annoying, but thank you for the reassurance." He extended both legs toward her. His feet were shod in shoes of identical make, but one was much larger than the other. "When she said I needed more lessons, I agreed that I needed a life-time's worth."

"You weren't that bad." She still felt as if she were pounding up the stairs to the ballroom, knowing she was missing something but not sure what.

"Ellie, for God's sake, I am being figurative." He sat up straight again. "Maybe. For this is the kernel of all the sense and all the realizations I've had knocked into my head: there is no one dearer to me than you, and I wish for nothing more than your happiness. The form that will take is for you and you alone to decide." He took a deep breath. "I am sorry that I kissed you before the eyes of society, because I do not wish to embarrass you. I am sorry I spoke as though I doubted your judgment, for in truth I do not. I will support you in your marriage to Barberry. I hope he will love you as you deserve."

Ah. As he spoke, her heart hammered, flipped, engaged in other strenuous activities—and then thumped heavily, chastened. "That is what you wish for me?"

"Yes. I wish your happiness."

"Thank you for your kind speech, but my happiness won't come from Lord Barberry." She cast her gaze downward. Her hands, still ringless, were strong. "I broke off the engagement to him. When he arrived at Athelney Place to escort me here, we...mutually agreed that we would not suit."

Poor man. He had looked so puzzled at the sight of her, with her hair bound and pinned up, but still curling riotously. "Are you unprepared?" he had asked. And she had said no, that she was perfectly ready.

He had understood at once. Their engagement was dissolved with the same courtesy with which it had been formed.

She stood from her chair, then paced the small distance to Nicholas and back. "I am not so eager for a husband that I will take just any, as it turns out. I want a loving family, but I have that already. Just not in the form I expected."

Sidney. Little Siddy. Mariah. Even, she thought, Nicholas. Perhaps someday his wife, if he wed someone pleasant. It was a good full life. She would find ways to be happy in it.

Nicholas's reply came after a long silence. "I didn't know you were no longer engaged. This... changes rather a lot."

The firelight in the otherwise dim room made her eyes water. "I realize that. Otherwise, your ridiculous gesture of support would have gone undone. As it is, I am sorry it was wasted."

"Ellie!" Did he *roll his eyes* at her? "It was never wasted. Had I known you and Barberry were no longer planning to wed, I'd have dragged you into this parlor at once instead of forcing a room full of people to endure me playing *I Sowed the Seeds of Love.* I shall have to apologize to the lot of them."

She was still missing something. "All right. You have wished me happy... I think. Do you not want to learn to play the pianoforte?"

"I have always wanted to learn. And if you'll teach me, I'd be honored. If that's all you want of me, I'll understand. And if—"

"Shh. Shh. You are babbling. What do you really want to tell me?"

"Ah. That." He looked abashed. "As it turns out"—he echoed her words—"I am not so eager for a wife that I will take just any."

Her heart was a boulder.

"My parents had a dutiful marriage. They probably thought, when they wed, that it would be perfect. But it was often contentious and unhappy."

"I remember." So many times, she and Sidney had walked over to his family home to play, only to walk right back to their own house with him.

"From them I learned that family life will inevitably be disappointing, so you might as well do whatever you want."

"I have never heard such sentiments from you before," she teased. "You, a duke, doing what you wish?"

"Such sarcasm!" He tilted his head. "It suits you. Minx."

She lifted her brows. "So, what of your courtship of Miss Lewis? If you're not eager for a wife, then she is…"

"Happily in the arms of Lord Barberry's eldest son, if my servants' gossip is to be trusted."

"Servants' gossip is always to be trusted." She plumped into her chair again.

"If so, then the lady was observed—by Lord Barberry's servants—to meet his heir's eyes and smile, which is more than she ever did for me."

"A shame." It was not a shame. "I was proud of having found you someone perfect, all blonde and blue-eyed and meek."

She was not proud of this. She had regretted it almost at once. But she valued Nicholas's happiness, just as he said he did hers.

He did not reply for a long while. When she looked at him curiously, she noticed a tremor in his hands. "That is not perfection to me." He steepled his hands beneath his chin, then drew in a deep breath. "I find that I prefer green eyes and brown hair. Brown with a hint of red in it, that looks rich and wild by the light of a candle and like spun copper under the noon sun. But it is not the green eyes and the brown hair that I truly prefer. It is the lady who possesses those features."

The lady who...

He meant...

Her heart, her breath, even the very fire, all seemed to pause.

"I..." She trailed off. Tried again. "Say some more things like that."

Did her hair really look like copper? Was it rich and appealing? Just now, it seemed a weight on her head, keeping her from thinking straight.

"There is but one more thing to say. I love you."

The fire gave a cheery snap. Her heart cautiously beat. Her breath was still caught. "As... as a friend, you mean? A life-long friend? Whose happiness you value?" This was her comeuppance for toying with the truth of her feelings when he'd asked.

"No." He dragged his hand through his hair. "That is—yes, but as more than that too. As a man loves the woman who is the better half of his heart. The claws don't matter anymore, because I'm not empty in the middle."

Deeply, slowly, she let out her breath. In the space left behind, bright joy began to grow. "I don't know what that bit about the claws means, but you say it as if it is quite a good thing."

"A very good thing. Very good indeed. I'll tell you all about it some other time, but for now just know that it's because of you. My love. When you started looking for a husband, I couldn't stop thinking about that. When you went out into the world, I couldn't stay away from your side. In short, I think you might be perfect for me, and I hope you'll entertain the possibility that I could be for you as well."

Her hands fluttered, as if trying to pluck his words from the air. Why was it so *dark* in here? She wanted noon light on him, full and strong, so she could read his every lineament. "I cannot believe it."

"Is it so hard to credit? You have always been essential to my happiness, and I hope I have given you some as well. For so long, I have loved you; I have just been too much of a fool to realize it."

"Dukes," she said faintly, "can be fools sometimes."

"They can. I freely admit it. I will never deny that again." He held out his arms to her then, and she all but flew into his lap.

"You said a great many things," she said. "I have only a few words in reply. I love you, and I think I always have."

"Thank God for that," he said.

Thereafter, the two of them discovered that this was not only the sort of space in which Eleanor might take her hair down and shake it free. It was also the sort of space where a man—a dear, clever, strange, and wonderful man—might loosen his cravat, take her in his arms, and become her lover.

Sort of. As best as one could become a lover in a chair made for one, while he had an injured ankle. The possibilities were limited but intriguing, and Nicholas was relentless. There were whispers, laughter, and kisses after kisses; then the shifting of clothing by questing hands. Pleasure quieted their voices, brought them together new and delighted, until it all tightened into a glorious burst and Eleanor collapsed against his chest with a soft cry.

They were both breathing hard. Together. Heartbeat against heartbeat, they settled into an embrace that felt, to Eleanor, like the embodiment of love.

She caught her breath first, though raggedly. "We must try this again on a larger piece of furniture."

"And soon, I hope." Nicholas stroked her back, currently covered by a very loosened bodice. "This is not a good beginning to convincing you that I can be proper and responsible."

"You are most responsible! I have never doubted your fitness as a duke for a moment."

"And as a lover?" Oh, that wicked twinkle in his eye.

She blushed furiously. "I am impressed by my experience so far."

"I am not too scandalous, as you once called me?"

She pretended to think about this. "You love me?"

"I love you."

"And you respect me?"

"Enough to make sure the door was latched before I put my hands up under your skirts."

She laughed, helpless at the force of her joy. "Then that is precisely the right amount of scandal. Let's wed as soon as we can get a license, and I shall be your scandalous duchess."

BCPL
Baltimore County
Public Library

About Theresa Romain

Theresa Romain is the bestselling author of historical romances, including the Matchmaker trilogy, the Holiday Pleasures series, the Royal Rewards series, and the Romance of the Turf trilogy. Praised as "one of the rising stars of Regency historical romance" (Booklist), she has received a starred review from Booklist and was a 2016 RITA® finalist. A member of Romance Writers of America® and its Regency specialty chapter The Beau Monde, Theresa is hard at work on her next novel from her home in the Midwest. Please visit her website at theresaromain.com, or find her on Facebook, Twitter, or Pinterest.

Books by Theresa Romain

Royal Rewards

Fortune Favors the Wicked

Passion Favors the Bold

Romance of the Turf

The Sport of Baronets (novella)

A Gentleman's Game

Scandalous Ever After

Stand-Alone Works

A Gentleman for All Seasons (anthology)

Those Autumn Nights (novella reissue)

My Scandalous Duke (novella)

The Matchmaker Trilogy
It Takes Two to Tangle
To Charm a Naughty Countess
Secrets of a Scandalous Heiress

Holiday Pleasures
Season for Temptation
Season for Surrender
Season for Scandal
Season for Desire